About the Author

Grahame Howard was born in London in 1953. He was brought up in Norwich, then returned to London to study medicine at St Thomas' Hospital Medical School. Following a series of junior doctor posts in London and Cambridge, he was appointed consultant clinical oncologist in 1986.

Set in 1970's London this is the second book in a trilogy featuring Andy Norris and his hapless friends.

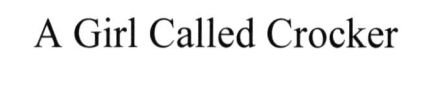

A Girl Called Crocker

Grahame C. W. Howard

A Girl Called Crocker

Vanguard Press

Dedication

For Rudi, Luke and Ollie

VANGUARD PAPERBACK

© Copyright 2025
Grahame C. W. Howard

The right of Grahame C. W. Howard to be identified as author of
this work has been asserted by him in accordance with the
Copyright, Designs and Patents Act 1988.

All Rights Reserved

No reproduction, copy or transmission of this publication
may be made without written permission.
No paragraph of this publication may be reproduced,
copied or transmitted save with the written permission of the
publisher, or in accordance with the provisions
of the Copyright Act 1956 (as amended).

Any person who commits any unauthorised act in relation to
this publication may be liable to criminal
prosecution and civil claims for damages.

A CIP catalogue record for this title is
available from the British Library.

ISBN 978 1 80016 775 9

This is a work of fiction. Names, characters, businesses, places, events and
incidents are either the product of the author's imagination or are used in a
fictitious manner. Any resemblance to actual persons, living or dead, or
actual events is purely coincidental.

*Vanguard Press is an imprint of
Pegasus Elliot Mackenzie Publishers Ltd.*
www.pegasuspublishers.com

First Published in 2025

**Vanguard Press
Sheraton House Castle Park
Cambridge England**

Printed & Bound in Great Britain

PROLOGUE

PC Crocker was shaking. Shaking uncontrollably with fear. To even the most casual observer, his appearance could hardly be described as anything but bizarre. He was wearing a short, black cocktail dress and in his lap, clutched firmly with both hands, was a small, red, shiny plastic handbag. Below the hem of his skirt his stockinged legs were visible, splayed in a rather unladylike fashion, while his knees, which could only be described as knobbly, were trembling. He was sitting rather primly on the edge of a red velvet settee, placed close to a large double bed in a dimly lit, seductively furnished boudoir.

It was stiflingly hot in the bedroom of the large Victorian mansion, and drips of sweat trickled from PC Crocker's underarms into his brassiere, which contained dusters to give the illusion of breasts. Underneath his long blonde wig, his scalp itched so much he could barely resist the overwhelming desire to remove it to scratch his head, and he suspected his make-up was beginning to run. He tried to think, but couldn't. He was aware that in dangerous situations like this a cool, calm head and ice-cold reasoning were essential, but, try as he might, all he could do was shake and whimper, rather than formulate a cogent strategy as to how to escape from the situation that he now found himself in. He knew that any moment now the game would be up and his cover blown. As soon as the man, who was currently washing in the en-suite bathroom, discovered his true identity, he, PC Crocker, was as good as dead. Odd, seemingly random thoughts shot through his mind like firecrackers on a dark night. 'I'm going to die, be murdered like Rosie,' he thought to himself. The man in the bathroom was now urinating noisily. 'When he finds out I'm a man, he'll kill me,' thought the policeman. Then Crocker considered, 'Maybe he's a homosexual. Oh *no*, that would be worse. How on earth have I managed to get myself into this mess?' he pondered. Then it occurred to him how ironic it was that, although throughout his whole life he had been chronically unable to attract a mate from the opposite sex, it appeared that he had now endeared himself to a member of the same sex. 'How on earth hasn't he realised that I'm a man?' he said quietly to himself. Crocker began to hyperventilate and became slightly dizzy. 'Calm down. Calm down,' he whispered. 'Remember your training.'

Crocker took a couple of deep breaths and began to search in the little handbag for something useful to defend himself with, but all he could find was an advert for a firm of dry cleaners and a tampon. He looked wistfully at the locked bedroom door and it was then that he heard the toilet flush and the door of the en-suite bathroom open. From within emerged a muscular man with biceps the size of Crocker's thighs and hands like spades. He was ruggedly handsome, in a coarse, unrefined kind of way, his short fair hair slicked down neatly with Brylcreem. He was wearing only jeans as he had removed his shirt – much of which had been stained a deep red – revealing a muscular torso and taut abdomen. A heavy gold chain hung about his neck, while several tattoos decorated his forearms.

The man looked at the luckless policeman seated nervously on the edge of the settee. 'Now, Fleur,' he murmured endearingly, 'I think you know why I've brought you up here.' He then advanced across the room to where PC Crocker sat whimpering, nervously fingering his handbag.

ONE

'What d'you want, Zeph?' Andy Norris lifted his gaze from the jukebox to his acquaintance, Zephaniah, who was seated at a table reading the *Racing Times*. They were in the Herald Lounge Bar, a rather soulless hostelry in the heart of the City of London.

'I don' care, man, so long as it ain't Mrs Mills.' Zephaniah chuckled in that deep-throated way that only those of Afro-Caribbean extraction can.

'*Mrs Mills Plays Christmas Tunes* hasn't been on the jukebox for the last two years,' Andy replied while studying the record list.

'I know, man, but I jus' worry that you might find a copy and put it on jus' so's you can annoy me. You know I hate that jingly bell thing.' Zephaniah shook his head in disgust. Andy pressed some buttons, there was a whirring noise from the machine and eventually the silence in the bar was shattered by the sound of Paul Simon telling anyone who was listening that there were fifty ways to leave a lover.

It was 1977, three years after Andrew Norris had survived an assassination attempt purely because the batter in which his piece of plaice had been deep-fried was ever so slightly soggier than usual. That alarming episode had briefly made him re-evaluate his life – to search for some meaning to his existence; to acquire some goals and ambitions. However, he had failed to do so, and this period of self-examination rapidly petered out, so that only a few weeks after the event he had reverted to his previous direction-less lifestyle. True, he had attempted to seduce Lucy, his housemate, but once again had been rebuffed, and now he had slipped back into his old, ambition-free existence. He still existed largely on fish and chips supplemented by liberal quantities of beer. It's fair to say he had converted to the healthier Embassy Regal cigarettes and had cut down to thirty a day, but what irked him most was that he still hadn't achieved his long-standing goal of a 170 three-dart checkout. He was, if anything, more obese than at the time of those momentous events of 1974, his hair just as unkempt, while his face as friendly yet vacant, as it had always been. He had been elevated to head of IT at Global Insurance, but that wasn't because he had been promoted: it was just that a more junior member of staff had been appointed to help him manage the ever-increasing amount of technology necessary to run a large insurance business.

After work each day he still frequented the Herald Lounge Bar, which, with its tacky plastic fittings, its mirrors and torn seats, had nothing to recommend it apart from its close vicinity to Andy's place of work. There he would read the *London Evening News* while consuming five or six pints of lager and occasionally swapping comments with Zephaniah, the night porter and the security officer at Global Insurance. At about eight thirty, he would proceed to Bank Tube Station, where he boarded a southbound tube train to Clapham Common. There, if he remembered to get off in time, he would buy a large portion of plaice and chips from the North Sea Fish Bar, which, in clement weather, he would consume while sitting on his favourite park bench on the edge of the Common, before finally returning to Parkview, where he shared a house with Lucy and a young doctor.

Having fuelled the jukebox with ten-pence pieces, Andy sat down, lit a cigarette and unfolded his newspaper. 'Bloody hell!' he exclaimed.

Zephaniah pushed his cloth cap back on his head and continued to peer studiously at the runners in the two thirty at Newmarket.

'Inflation's running at twenty-seven percent!' Andy looked at the man sitting next to him. The middle-aged security officer had changed little over the years that Andy had been drinking with him. Every evening, as regular as clockwork, he sat in the bar, where he picked his losers, as he called them (which they invariably were). Then, just before eight o'clock, he would leave to start his night shift at Global Insurance.

'Zeph, did you hear me? Inflation is a staggering *twenty-seven* percent!'

'I heard you, man.'

'That's ridiculous. It can't go on like this. D'you realise that the price of this drink,' and he raised his pint of lager to illustrate his point, 'has gone up...' Andy's eyes screwed up for a moment as he concentrated, 'about twelve pence by my reckoning.' Andy took a sip of the precious liquid. 'Or to put it another way, I get twenty percent less each time I buy a pint.' He looked up at the ceiling. 'No, that's not right, but you know what I mean.'

'That's why I drink rum and Coke, man.'

Andy looked at Zephaniah, a puzzled expression on his face. 'But, Zeph, you've missed the point; it doesn't matter what...' But then, thinking better of it, he paused and sighed, 'Oh, it doesn't matter. Anyway, the thing is, I reckon I could make a better job of running the country than this bunch of Muppets.'

'Good show.'

'What d'you mean, "Good show"?'

'Good show – the Muppets. My favourite is Miss Piggy.'

Elton John and Kiki Dee wailed out from the jukebox something about breaking each other's hearts.

After a moment Zephaniah added, 'Why don' you then?' before carefully circling the name of a horse with his red crayon.

'Why don't I do what?'

'Run the country, man.'

'Maybe I should.' Andy thought for a moment. 'I could stand for the Beer and Darts Party.'

'Bad party,' Zephaniah responded without looking up from his paper.

'What d'you mean it's a bad party?' asked Andy.

Zeph sighed and put his paper down on the table in front of him. 'Bad party. B–A–D. Beer – and – darts. Geddit?'

Andy looked skywards. 'Ah yes, I see. Quite a good acronym actually. We would need to have a manifesto.' Andy was thoughtful. 'How about...' – he hesitated for a moment – 'all pubs should serve real ale and darts teams must practice at least twice a week? That would get us votes.'

'Dream on, man.'

Suddenly, Andy sat bolt upright and peered more closely at his newspaper. 'Here, Zeph. You'll never guess what. The body of a young woman has been found on Clapham Common.' Andy, a hint of animation on his normally vacuous face, glanced at Zephaniah.

Zephaniah's eyes widened and his jaw dropped. 'Oh no! It's you, man. You is bad news. Was you next to her when she was killed. It ain't safe bein' next to you. I'm surprised I lived this long, man.'

Zephaniah was referring to the little unpleasantness two years before when a tramp sitting next to Andy while he was eating fish and chips on his favourite park bench on Clapham Common, was unexpectedly shot dead.

'Calm down, Zeph. This is the first I've heard of it. I was nowhere near at the time. However, Clapham

Common does seem to be a bit dangerous, I'd agree.'

Andy read out loud from the newspaper. 'The body of a woman in her late twenties was found on Clapham Common in the early hours of yesterday morning. Police consider the death to be suspicious and are pursuing several lines of enquiry. They have issued an appeal for witnesses.'

'That means they haven't got a clue.'

'Probably,' said Andy, recalling the investigation by PC Crocker and the Chief Superintendent two years before, when he was persuaded to act as a decoy to catch a gangster called Kenny 'The Giant' Craft.

TWO

'Take a seat, Crocker.' The Chief Superintendent, who had been sitting looking at a photograph of his passing-out parade which hung on the wall of his office, then swivelled his chair so violently that he gyrated too far and ended up facing the opposite wall. He swung his seat back, this time halting directly in front of Crocker. Now stationary but feeling slightly dizzy, the Chief shook his head before indicating the vacant chair on the opposite side of his desk.

'Thank you, sir,' replied Crocker, who then advanced timidly across the Chief Super's office.

'Bowels okay?'

'Yes, thank you, sir.'

'Good. You can't police with irregular bowels, I always say. Regularity is paramount if you're going to catch criminals.' The Chief Super looked at Crocker sternly. 'What's paramount?'

'Regularity, sir.'

'Absolutely right. But we're not here to talk about matters peristaltic, important though they are. No, Crocker, I want to know about the stolen bike. You know the one I mean?'

'Yes, sir. I remember it well. Silver frame, drop handlebars and pink mudguards. Quite distinctive as I recall.'

'Absolutely. Have you found it yet?'

'Well, not exactly, sir.'

'How do you mean, "not exactly"?'

'Well – not at all, really, sir.'

'That's more "not at all" than "not exactly", isn't it, Crocker? Are you sure you're regular.'

'Absolutely, sir.'

'Any idea why this bicycle has proved to be so elusive?'

'Difficult to say, sir. I was wondering if it had been resprayed or perhaps disguised in some way.'

'For heaven's sake, Crocker, disguised as what – a *jumbo* jet?' The Chief sighed before continuing. 'What *have* you been doing these last two years? On second thoughts, don't answer that.' The Chief sat back in his swivel chair, put his fingertips together and looked at the ceiling thoughtfully. 'At least you did help out with the attempted assassination of that idiot, what's-his-name?'

'Norris, sir.'

'What?' The Chief peered at Crocker with a puzzled expression.

'Norris. Andy Norris – that was the name of what's-his-name.'

'Yes, I remember now. You caught the criminal while cunningly disguised, as I recall.'

'Yes, sir. I was a Scout Leader. I think I have a bit of a talent for undercover work, even if I say so myself.'

'Yes. Your Scouting disguise was inspirational.'

'Thank you, sir.'

'Well, Crocker, the reason I've got you up here today is because I think we might be in need of your undercover skills again.'

'Oh, good, sir.'

'Yes. It's about that girl, Rosie Little: the one who was found dead on the Common. We believe that she was murdered.'

Crocker tilted his head and looked at his senior with what was meant to be an intelligent expression, but which only made him look more vacuous than usual and ever so slightly simple.

'Between you and me, Crocker, we have no leads whatsoever, although we haven't told the press that, of course. They think we're close to a breakthrough, which is not entirely accurate.'

'Mmm, sir.'

'I have been approached by a lady, a charming lady actually – no bowel problems there, I'm sure,' the Chief added as an aside, 'who runs the guesthouse where the girl was staying. She feels that one of her male clients,' the Chief coughed, 'by which I mean staff – of course – might have had something to do with it.'

'Shall I go down and investigate, sir? Sniff around.'

'No.' The Chief Super coughed again and looked at the wall. 'The whole situation is rather sensitive – can't say why – classified, you know. An open approach is just not possible: hence the need for discretion. Your undercover skills will be vital. What we need here is subterfuge, Crocker. What do we need?'

'Subterfuge, sir.'

'Precisely. Bang on.'

Crocker was now beginning to get quite excited about his new rôle. 'I think the Scout Leader disguise would be ideal, sir. People open up to a Boy Scout in a way they don't to other members of society.'

'No! That's not possible, Crocker.'

PC Crocker frowned for a moment, then his face lit up with inspiration. 'Well, how about a man of the cloth, then? That should do it.'

'No. Not possible. In fact, that's an even worse idea.'

PC Crocker looked bemused. Two of his best disguises had been turned down without any serious consideration whatsoever.

The Chief continued, 'You'll have to be disguised as a woman.'

Crocker looked as though he had been run over by a train. His jaw dropped as far as was anatomically possible, making his wobbling uvula visible to anyone who might have been looking into his mouth, while his eyes widened, giving him a staring, demented appearance. He remained that way for several seconds while his mind attempted to comprehend what his superior had just said. He tried to speak, but he could only produce spluttering noises and grunts. Eventually, after several seconds, he regained control of his vocal cords and shouted, '*A woman?*'

'Yes, Crocker. A woman. You know, one of those things that walk around in skirts.'

'But!'

'A woman it has to be, Crocker.'

'B-but why?'

The Chief coughed again and looked at the ceiling. 'It seems that Ivy...' The Chief Super checked himself and coughed again. 'That is – the delightful lady who is the proprietress of the guest house – only allows female guests.'

Crocker was still having trouble controlling his voice and for a while could only emit strange whistling sounds. Eventually, he stuttered, 'S-so this is a g-guest house for w-w-women only?'

'Precisely.'

'Er – except for one man who might be the killer.'

'Spot on, Crocker. Good to see you've not lost your touch. Now off you go; and remember, keep regular.'

To say that Crocker was disturbed by the interview would be an understatement. He didn't even vaguely understand his brief. It seemed that he was to dress as a woman and stay in a guesthouse for women only (the one where Rosie Little had last been seen alive) where a member of staff was suspected of murdering her. Even to his less than astute mind the details and reasoning behind the operation seemed to be sketchy.

Nonetheless, he rather relished the idea of going undercover once more, and a successful outcome might mean promotion. He was, quite naturally, ever so slightly concerned about the particular problems associated with dressing as a woman, but over the next few days Crocker set about procuring the necessary items of clothing with considerable enthusiasm.

Initially, he went to a small clothes shop in Clapham, but after some disturbing interchanges with a salesman who appeared to be wearing lipstick and eyeshadow, he decided to do his shopping at an Oxfam shop, where no one seemed at all interested in what he bought. Back in his small flat, after locking the door and closing the curtains, he donned the dresses, stockings and other female paraphernalia he had acquired, put on a wig, applied some make-up and practised being a woman. After three days, he felt confident in his disguise and knew that the next test of how convincing it was would have to be outside the confines of his bedroom.

THREE

'Lucy.' There was no answer, so Andy Norris turned to face the open hatch in the wall between the kitchen and the lounge, where he was lying in his customary supine position on the settee. '*Lucy,*' he shouted. 'I know you're there. Make us a coffee, would you?'

'You're a lazy bastard, Andy Norris,' came a voice from the kitchen.

'I know. Five sugars, please.' Andy settled back on the settee and opened his copy of the *London Evening News*. It was nine o'clock in the evening and he had just returned from the Herald Lounge Bar via the park bench on the edge of Clapham Common, where he liked to eat his fish and chips. He was now ready for a post-prandial coffee.

Lucy kicked the door open and entered the lounge carrying two steaming mugs. A pretty if slightly plump girl in her late twenties, she was in her dressing gown and her freshly washed hair was wrapped in a towelling turban. ''Ere you are,' she said, passing one of the mugs over, before slumping into a comfy chair and peering at the TV.

'Thanks, Luce.' Andy took a sip of coffee.

'Sweet enough?' asked Lucy.

'Yes thanks, and you?'

'Ha, ha.'

'Lucy, did you know there's been a murder on the Common?'

'Yeah, I 'eard. Nowhere's safe nowadays.'

'Well, you should be careful. If I were you, I wouldn't cross the Common alone.'

''Ow d'you expect me to get 'ome, then? Walk two miles round it?'

'Seriously, Lucy. You should be careful. If anything happened to you I'd have to make my own coffee.'

Lucy was silent for a moment. 'Was this girl sitting next to you by any chance, Andy Norris. I'm beginning to wonder about you. The last time someone was killed around 'ere, it was your fault.'

'Not *you* as well! It wasn't my fault that tramp was killed. It was just a case of mistaken identity.'

'Well, that's clearly not the case this time. No one could mistake a fat bastard like you for a pretty young girl.'

'I'm not a fat bastard – I'm simply well-nourished.'

'Well-nourished, fat bastard, it's all the same to me.'

'What you need, Lucy, is the protection of a man, and I'm volunteering for the job.'

'I wouldn't be seen dead out with you.'

'That's the point: you wouldn't *be* dead if you were out with me.'

Andy had tried to date Lucy for nearly three years now without success. He had on occasions taken her out for a drink at one of the local pubs where he played darts, but the relationship had always been platonic, and the more he failed in his attempts to seduce her, the more he was attracted to her. Since she had sacked Nigel Bernard-Fielding, the imposter whom Andy had called Twatface, she had rattled through half a dozen unsuccessful relationships. A secretary at a local law firm who wanted more from life than marriage to one of the local boys, with the inevitable drudgery of children and a mortgage. She wanted adventure and romance. Andy also knew this and realised that he represented neither. 'Fancy a beer this weekend?' he asked innocently. He knew that Lucy was between boyfriends and this might represent an opportunity for him to stake a claim to her affections.

Lucy was silent for a moment. 'Yeah, okay. I got nothing to do. 'Ow about Saturday?'

'Good! We'll go out in the evening. We could go to the Plough and then on to the Nellie. How does that sound?'

'You certainly know how to treat a girl, Andy Norris.'

The sarcasm did not register with Andy since, for him, nothing could be better than half a dozen pints in each of these pubs, followed by a large portion of fish and chips – except maybe the possibility of a 170 three-dart checkout. 'Great. I have to go into work Saturday morning, but will be back by two, so let's go out at about six o'clock.'

Andy planned the evening carefully. He reckoned a couple of drinks in the Plough would be a good start to the evening; then he would surprise Lucy by taking her to a restaurant. His idea of taking a girl out for a meal usually amounted to a packet of crisps or (on a special occasion) maybe a hot pie from the bar of one of the many pubs he frequented. A proper meal, in a restaurant, with a bottle of wine, maybe even some flowers should do the trick, he thought. However, like all Andy's projects, it didn't go quite according to plan. It might have been the mental strain of planning the evening that made him feel rather nervous, but for whatever reason he decided to go for a beer after he had finished work on the day in question. He rarely frequented the Herald Lounge Bar on a Saturday lunchtime and he was surprised to find several colleagues there. He got chatting to the other drinkers, one drink led to another, and by three o'clock Andy had consumed eight pints of lager. Surprised by the passage of time, he made his excuses and boarded the Tube to Clapham. It was just after four when he let himself into Parkview and was relieved to find that Lucy was out. He settled down on the settee, lit a cigarette and thought he would rest for a while before getting changed for the evening.

Lucy, meanwhile, was doing what she did best – shopping. She had travelled to Oxford Street and spent the afternoon trawling the shops for bargains. Lucy was a person who bought things because they were cheap, not because she needed or wanted them – often wondering as soon as she arrived home what she would do with her bargains. That day, she bought a woollen hat which was very cheap; she never wore hats, but thought she might wear this one. Then she purchased a mini-skirt which was far too small for her as it barely fitted over her hips, but she thought it would encourage her to lose weight and she liked the colour. Finally, she spotted some hooped earrings which she guessed might come in handy if she ever got her ears pierced. Back at Parkview, loaded down with shopping bags, she struggled to find her key and let herself in. Once inside, she noticed a strange smell and, looking along the hallway, saw a wisp of dark smoke emanating from the lounge. She dropped her bags, ran along the hall and threw open the lounge door. There, lying on the couch, sound asleep and snoring loudly, was Andy. Around him smoke was rising from the settee and his cigarette was still visible glowing on the cushion where it had fallen.

'*Andy*!' she shouted.

Andy, while under the influence of eight pints of lager, had fallen asleep as soon as he had sat down, and was totally oblivious to Lucy's shouting. It was only when she shook him vigorously that he opened his eyes, looked about and registered that something was not quite right.

'Funny smell in here, Lucy,' he said. Then, after looking around blearily for a moment, he suddenly noticed the smoke rising from all around him. Showing remarkable agility for an obese man with eight pints of lager on board, he suddenly leapt up from the settee and yelled, 'Shit, the house is on fire. Lucy, the house is on fire!'

'I *know*, it's the settee that's on fire.'

Andy was now standing next to the smouldering piece of furniture, staring at it in disbelief. 'How did that happen?'

'Andy, you fat bastard, you've set the bloody settee on fire.'

'I did not.'

'You did. Look! There's your cigarette.'

Suddenly, the situation dawned on Andy and he realised that he must have fallen asleep with a lighted cigarette, and now ever thicker and more pungent smoke was billowing out from the settee. 'Oh, shit. Quick, help me get it into the garden.'

The lounge had French doors which opened onto a small back garden, and Andy and Lucy between them somehow managed to push and pull the smoking couch into the relative safety of the garden, where, as soon as it was exposed to the gentle breeze, it burst into flames.

It was six thirty before the fire was extinguished and the crew, having lectured Andy on the dangers of falling asleep while smoking and drunk numerous cups of sweet tea served up by Lucy, finally took their leave. As the appliance drove away, Lucy stomped back into the house and along the hallway growling, '*Andy! Andy!*'

Andy, realising that this hadn't been the most auspicious start to a romantic evening, didn't immediately answer. He thought of trying to hide until Lucy's mood improved, but the events of the afternoon had affected his judgement and speed of cerebration adversely, so all he managed to do was to stand in the middle of the lounge and look vacant.

'*You drunken slob.*' Lucy stamped her foot, causing a splash from the carpet where one of the hoses used to extinguish the settee had leaked on to the floor. 'Andy Norris. *What were you thinking of?* You nearly got us killed.'

Andy was speechless. He had nowhere to sit, as the charred remains of his beloved settee were now dripping in the garden behind him, so he stood in the middle of the lounge, his belly hanging over his belt and dark pieces of burnt settee smeared liberally over his face and clothes.

Andy was aware that what he said next might have a profound effect on the rest of the evening, so he hesitated. He considered apologizing, but for some unknown reason decided against it. What he *did* say, he realised in later days, was possibly not the most appropriate response to Lucy's invective.

'Right, Lucy. I'll just have a quick wash and then we'll be getting off.'

Lucy was silent and simply walked towards him, looked him unflinchingly in the eye and then punched him as hard as she could in the stomach.

Andy was not too discomfited by this as he had plenty of flesh to absorb the blow. He looked at Lucy with a surprised and slightly hurt expression on his face. 'Ah, Lucy, don't you want to come out with me now?'

Lucy stood stock-still for a moment, before punching him again, harder. This time it did hurt, and Andy doubled up with pain. Eventually, between gasps, he managed to say, 'Okay. Maybe another time?' He looked up enquiringly at Lucy.

Lucy was now getting the hang of it and her third punch was a cracker, and when Andy got up off his knees, his worst fears had been confirmed. The date was now officially off and the odds of a successful seduction at any time in the foreseeable future were longer than ever.

FOUR

The following week, Crocker decided to try out his disguise. Although going undercover in an all-female guesthouse did not seem to him to represent a high-risk operation, he was a professional, and if he said he would disguise himself as a woman, then he would do so to the best of his ability. He had given careful consideration as to how he might best try out his disguise. He thought of simply walking the streets for a few hours, but realised that this might be misinterpreted, and if the situation arose where he did attract attention from the opposite (or rather the same) sex, it might prove to be difficult to extricate himself from such a situation without blowing his cover and thus putting the whole operation at risk. Then there was the possibility of being picked up by one of his own colleagues for soliciting – which would have been embarrassing to say the least. 'No,' he thought to himself, 'I'll put my disguise to the ultimate test in a safe environment.' Where better, he felt, than in his own police station, where, if it all went pear-shaped, he could come clean and his Chief Superintendent would corroborate the reason why he, PC Crocker, was dressed as a woman and behaving in a way that an unbiased observer might consider somewhat suspicious. He chose a day when he was officially off-duty so that no one would expect him to be at the station and a time when he knew that the Chief Super had no appointments.

He rose early, bathed, shaved his face and legs and started to don his disguise. He refused to wear women's knickers as he thought that was somehow perverted, so he put on his normal off-white Y-fronts and then, with some difficulty, strapped on a bra plumped out with several handkerchiefs. He carefully pulled on some tights and then a deep red blouse with puffed shoulders and frilly cuffs. For his skirt he had chosen a knee-length tweedy affair in autumn reds and greens. Although it was mid-summer, the only coat he could find which fitted him at the Oxfam shop was a light fawn mackintosh. He looked at himself in his bathroom mirror and realised that something was lacking. 'A necklace. That's what I need,' he said to himself. Amazingly, in an old suitcase under the bed he found exactly what he was looking for. His late mother's string of pearls. Shoes had been a real problem. For a man of his size he had quite large feet, and under the rather suspicious gaze of the assistant at the Oxfam shop, he had tried on many different pairs. Undoubtedly, the most appropriate would have been a pair of light-brown women's brogues, but in a moment of madness he considered these to be too frumpy and went for some red sling-backs with three-inch heels.

'Now for the difficult bit,' he thought, as he began to apply his make-up. Like most men, he knew nothing of the arcane skills of make-up application and made the mistake that all beginners do – he didn't know when to stop. Before he realised it, his bright red lips had spread ever wider and longer until they extended virtually from ear to ear and nose to chin, where they merged imperceptibly into the bright rouge which appeared to cover the rest of his face except for his forehead, which was white and sweaty. When he looked in the bathroom mirror, he gave himself a considerable shock, and with difficulty wiped it all off. Then he reapplied the make-up in exactly the same way with exactly the same result. At a third attempt, exercising considerable restraint and aware that he had nearly used up the entire contents of his newly purchased make-up bag, his facial colour scheme looked almost presentable. The final touch was a wig. The reader must remember that Crocker was not terribly *au fait* with the opposite sex and, so far as he was aware, all girls had long blonde hair. Hence, he adorned himself with long, sandy-coloured tresses which tumbled on to his shoulders and over the top of his blouse, which was tightly buttoned at the neck.

PC Crocker gazed at himself for one last time and, quite satisfied with his appearance, he popped his door keys in the pocket of his raincoat (he had neglected to purchase a handbag) closed the front door behind him and stepped out into the bright sunshine of the early summer's day. He then took a deep breath of refreshing summer air, turned to his right and strode purposefully (or as purposefully as he could in his new shoes) down the street in the general direction of the police station.

It is fair to say that he soon began to attract a considerable amount of attention. To the casual observer his appearance was unnatural – one of disarray, indeed of muddle. Crocker was short, with a slim frame, so that he didn't immediately look masculine, but there was something not quite right about his demeanour. It is possible that his stride was not sufficiently effeminate, or maybe it was the fact that he decided to have a quick cigarette as he walked, holding it in the palm of his hand in that very masculine way; yet, for whatever reason, somehow his *alter ego* was not convincing. At best he looked like a rather butch, tweedy, middle-aged prostitute; at worst like a policeman in drag. Nonetheless, he attracted some attention which he considered to be positive. An elderly man, who, perhaps significantly, was wearing glasses the lenses of which were the thickness of the bottom of milk bottles, looked at Crocker several times before smiling and doffing his trilby, while a group of young layabouts eyed him up and wolf-whistled as he walked past, while one of them shouted, 'Cor, don't arf fancy you, missus.'

All in all, Crocker was quite satisfied with progress as he leapt up the steps of the police station two at a time before throwing open the doors and approaching the desk sergeant.

'I'd like to see the Chief Superintendent, please,' he said authoritatively.

The desk sergeant, who had been concentrating on a newspaper laid out in front of him, raised his head slowly. 'D'you 'ave an appointment?' he asked, then he frowned and peered at Crocker for a moment, before adding, 'Miss.'

'No, but I'm sure he'll see me.'

'Who shall I say it is, miss?'

In the excitement of planning his disguise, Crocker had completely forgotten that his *alter ego* would need a name. His eyes widened and he gazed around the room for inspiration. The sergeant, who had his pencil licked and ready in hand, was now looking at Crocker with increasing suspicion. 'Your name, miss?' he repeated.

Crocker panicked and continued to stare at the floor and said the first word that came into his head. 'Floor,' he almost shouted.

The policeman smiled benignly. 'Fleur: nice name, miss. You take a seat over there now and I'll see if the Chief Super's available. Can I ask what it's about?'

Again Crocker hesitated, then, in as coquettish a way as he could manage, said, 'It's about a guesthouse – an all-female one.' Crocker winked at the policeman. 'He'll understand.'

The sergeant's eyes widened and his face reddened. 'Oh, I see. Certainly, miss. I'll just be a minute.'

Crocker took a seat and began to realise how unseasonally warm his clothes were. He was worried that his make-up might run but hadn't thought to bring a mirror or any of the other bits and pieces that women carry about with them at all times. So he sat, his legs rather inelegantly apart, and waited for the return of his colleague, reassured that he at least hadn't seen through the disguise.

After a couple of minutes, the sergeant returned and said in a somewhat surprised tone, 'The Chief Superintendent will see you immediately, miss.' He then escorted Crocker towards the door of the Chief's office, opened it and stood back reverentially to allow Crocker to enter. Once inside, the Chief, who was standing behind his desk, looked at him and smiled. 'Come on in, my dear. I don't think we've met before.'

Crocker was now in uncharted territory. He had intended to test his disguise and not only had it worked, in that neither the desk sergeant nor his Chief had recognised him, but both men's behaviour towards him had been unexpectedly polite and disconcertingly flirtatious. He wasn't sure whether or not to throw off his wig and shout, '*Fooled* you. It's *me*, PC Crocker,' or continue the charade for a while longer. In the event he said, 'No. Not to my knowledge.'

Then the Chief said something strange. 'Now, where's Ivy been hiding *you*?' The Chief leered at Crocker, his face a trifle more rubose than Crocker remembered from previous interviews. 'I say, Fleur, you're a cracker,' he continued.

'No, I'm—' Crocker was about to correct his senior, but was interrupted.

'Yes. Ivy must have been keeping you for a special occasion, I'd say. Do take a seat.' The Chief indicated the chair opposite him.

Crocker sat down rather inelegantly. You will remember that Crocker thus far had said nothing apart from denying that he'd met the Chief before, and here was the Chief Super talking to him as though they were old friends. Crocker was confused and could only listen as the Chief continued. 'So, Ivy sent you along to see how things were going, eh?' The Chief smiled and looked deep into Crocker's eyes. 'Well, you can tell her that it's all under control. I've put one of my best men on to the case – undercover. He'll be with you any day now to flush the killer out. Then, once he's flushed him out, things can get back to normal. Know what I mean?' The Chief looked at the ceiling wistfully. 'We'll flush, then flush again, and keep flushing until we've flushed him out.' The Chief Super then swung round in his swivel chair and once more looked Crocker straight in the eye. 'What'll we do, Fleur?'

'Flush, sir.' Crocker's reply had been reflex, and on hearing this familiar response, the Chief looked closely at the person sitting opposite him. 'I say, Fleur. It's not you, is it, Crocker?'

Crocker heaved a sigh of relief and tore off his wig like a conjurer plucking a rabbit out of a top hat. 'Yes, sir! It's me! It's me, PC Crocker. I thought I'd just try my disguise out on you, sir.'

The Chief was now redder than ever and coughed several times. 'I say, Crocker, I must say you had me going there for a bit. Jolly good disguise. Spot on. Of course I knew it was you and was just playing along to see how you coped.' The Chief coughed again. 'All of that stuff about... er...' He coughed again. 'Er, Ivy, was just me role-playing.'

'Of course, sir, all part of the subterfuge.'

'Absolutely, Crocker. Subterfuge. That's what we need, and we've got it in spadefuls. What have we got in spadefuls, Crocker?'

'Subterfuge, sir.'

'Absolutely. Well, I hope me playing along there taught you a thing or two, as next time you'll be on your own.'

'So you think the disguise is okay then, sir?'

'Spot on, Crocker. You even had me going for a moment, and I'm highly trained to detect deception. The ordinary man on the street or indeed in a...' The Chief hesitated. 'Er, guesthouse, wouldn't spot a thing.'

'Oh, good, sir. I thought I had a bit of a talent for this sort of work.'

'You get on down to the guesthouse and sniff about a bit. Flush him out, Crocker, flush him out.'

'Certainly, sir.'

'Right, off you go and remember, *flush* is the word.'

'Yes, sir.' Crocker rose and turned to go, but in his excitement forgot his wig, which was lying on the desk in front of the Chief Super.

'Crocker,' said the Chief.

'Yes, sir?' Crocker turned to look at the Chief.

'Haven't you forgotten something?'

'Sir?' The Chief looked at the wig lying in front of him. 'Oh, thanks, sir,' and Crocker hastily replaced the wig and marched out of the office, closing the door behind him. As he walked past the desk sergeant, he smiled and said, 'Thanks, Sarge,' then pouted his lips.

The policeman raised his eyebrows, reddened ever so slightly, before replying, 'A pleasure, Fleur. Any time.'

Crocker, encouraged by the success of his disguise, had now become somewhat over-confident. With one last backward glance at the sergeant, he flung open the door of the police station and strode briskly through. As any female reader will know, high heels and striding are not natural bedfellows, and the inevitable happened – the unexpected strain resulted in one of the heels becoming detached from the rest of the shoe, causing Crocker to tumble headlong down the stone steps, where he landed in a crumpled heap at the bottom. He lay there for a moment, slightly dazed, until an elderly lady came and helped him to his feet.

'Are you all right, dear?' she enquired, peering at Crocker's wig, which was now sitting at an alarming angle on the side of his head.

'Yes, fine. Thank you,' replied Crocker, straightening his headgear. 'Must have slipped on the top step.'

The old lady dropped her gaze to Crocker's feet. 'If I was you, dear, I'd stick to low heels in future.'

FIVE

'Andy.' Lucy looked at her housemate with an expression that can only be described as disdain. 'If I had my way, I wouldn't even pass on this invitation, but Lucinda insisted. For some bizarre reason, she seems to think you're a – what she calls a "good egg".'

'You haven't told her about the little unpleasantness of the flaming settee, have you?' asked Andy, who was perched uncomfortably on a tall bar stool which was placed in the middle of the lounge at Parkview. After the demise of the settee, Lucy had refused to allow him to replace it with another, and insisted that he now sat on this stool at all times. Her logic was that it required a modicum of sobriety to remain balanced upon it, and if he began to doze off with a lit cigarette he would fall, thereby waking himself up before he could set the house on fire again. As far as she was concerned, it was an essential precaution for the safety of all in the household.

'Yeah, I did,' replied Lucy. 'I 'oped that when I told 'er you 'ad a penchant for setting 'ouses on fire, she would then see sense and refuse to have you within a hundred miles of her mansion; but for some reason she thought the whole episode was 'ilarious.'

'I always knew Lucinda had good taste. I hope you told her that I would be delighted to attend her house-party?'

'No! I said you were busy and wouldn't be able to go.'

'That's not fair,' exclaimed Andy. 'It's the first invitation I've had for years.'

'Well, as it 'appens, she was so disappointed when I said you couldn't go that she asked me to try to persuade you to change your mind.'

'But how can I change my mind when I haven't refused in the first place?'

'Don't confuse me; if I 'ad my way I wouldn't ask you at all, but I promised.'

Andy smiled at Lucy. 'You see, Lucy, someone thinks I'm good company.'

'It's nothing to do with being good company, Andy Norris. It's simply because she thinks that you are at least partially responsible for getting Rupert to propose to her.'

'But as I understand it, he didn't.'

'No. Well, not exactly, but he doesn't know that, and you mustn't tell him.' Lucy was referring to the night when Andy and Lucy had shown Lucinda and Rupert around a selection of Clapham hostelries, following which Lucinda persuaded Rupert that he had proposed to her and she had accepted.

Andy rearranged his backside on the bar stool and lit a cigarette. 'So I did her a good turn. Tell her, if you would, that I would be delighted to accept her kind invitation and, Lucy, I would be pleased to escort you.'

'You're not coming nowhere near me, let alone escorting me,' said Lucy vehemently. 'It's dangerous being anywhere in your vicinity.'

'Okay, but we might as well travel up there together.'

It was a month after the little unpleasantness of the burning settee, and Andy had detected no sign of a thaw between Lucy and himself. In fact, all communication had been monosyllabic, and this was the nearest they had come to a conversation since that event. Andy was delighted, as he felt this was an opportunity to shine in Lucy's presence. All he had to do was to appear urbane and debonair for three days and Lucy might, just might, see him in a more favourable light. He knew this was not going to be easy since being urbane and debonair did not come naturally to Andy Norris. Being fat and pissed were more his style, but he was determined to give it his best shot.

***

'So, Zeph, this is it. This is the weekend.'
   'The weekend for what, man?'
   'The weekend for seducing the lovely Lucy.'
   'What you on about, Andy?'

'Zeph, my dear old chap, this is the weekend when Lucy is going to see a different me – an urbane man of the world. A new, exciting, supercharged Andy Norris.'

Andy, the jukebox freshly reloaded, had just sat down next to his friend Zephaniah, as the Starland Vocal Band extolled the pleasures of some afternoon delight. He lit a cigarette and took a long gulp from his pint of lager.

'How is you goin' to be urban and stuff?' Zephaniah looked up from his copy of the *Racing Times*. 'That's just not you, man.'

'It's *urbane*, Zeph, not urban.' Andy sat back in his chair and blew a cloud of smoke towards the ceiling of the Herald Lounge Bar. 'I've received an invitation requesting the pleasure of my company at a weekend house-party at Warren Hall, the country seat of the fourteenth Earl of...' Andy paused for a moment, his brow creased in thought. 'Somewhere – Rupert what's-his-face, and I'm taking Lucy along.'

'I thought she wasn't talking to you since you set her on fire?'

'I didn't set her on fire, Zeph. The settee that I was lying on, pretending to be asleep, happened to spontaneously combust. But you're right, for a while the shine did go off our relationship; but now I'm confident it's as bright as ever.'

Zeph raised a red crayon above the open page of the *Sporting World*, closed his eyes and brought it down with a sharp jerk. He opened his eyes to see where the pen had landed. 'Oh no, man, I've just bought a new television.'

'What do you mean?' Andy looked up from his copy of the *London Evening News*, puzzled.

'It's the new system for choosing my losers. I just close my eyes and jab my crayon on to the paper, and the nearest horse is the one I bet on. It's better than me choosing and saves time, only this time I've hit a television advert.'

Andy shook his head and looked down at his paper. 'I see they've not found the murderer.'

'What murderer?'

'The person that killed the young girl on Clapham Common. They've identified her as Rosie Little. Apparently, she had a head injury. It suggests here that she might have been a prostitute.'

'Where was you that night, man? That's what I want to know.'

'I keep telling you, Zeph, that this murder is nothing to do with me. Although I do wonder if the same team of incompetent nonces that nearly got me killed three years ago are the ones who are investigating this crime. It says here that the police are following up several lines of enquiry.'

'That means they don' have a clue, man.'

There was silence in the bar for a while, then Zephaniah laid his paper on the table and looked at Andy. 'You said you was goin' to be a councillor, man. Bring a bit of law an' order to the borough. Whatever happened to that plan? You bein' Wyatt Earp to my Doc Holliday.'

'That would certainly impress Lucy,' replied Andy, looking wistfully into the distance.

'You was goin' to be the BAD Party candidate.'

'Yes. But I'd need a seat to contest. There would have to be a vacancy for me to stand.'

'Wot you mean?'

'Well, as I understand it, if there is a vacancy – that is, if an incumbent member of the council resigns or dies or something – then there is a by-election and anyone can stand as an Independent candidate. You need an agent, then you complete a set of forms, pay a deposit and Bob's your uncle, you're a candidate.'

Zephaniah thought for a moment. 'I'll be your agent, man. I always fancied being a secret agent.'

'No, Zeph, this is a different type of agent.'

'I know – this is a *BAD* agent. I is your man for that job.'

'Zeph, you're digressing. I was talking about my forthcoming seduction of the lovely Lucy.'

'Good luck to you, man. Personally, I think you're better off unmarried. By the way, I just got married again.'

Andy looked up, surprised at the unexpected news. 'What? You've got married again? You've already got several wives! What was it? Three at the last count?'

'No. One left so there was a vacancy. I got a replacement to maintain the *status quo*.'

'Well, Zeph, you amaze me, but I have to go. I won't be in on Friday as I'll be on my way to the country, so wish me luck. I'm off.' So saying, Andy rose from his seat and prepared to leave.

'But, Andy, it's only seven thirty and you're still sober. You've only had three pints, man. Is you ill?'

'No, Zeph, it's the new me. I told you, the finely honed, urbane Andrew Norris.'

'But it's my round, man.'

Andy hesitated for just a moment before saying, 'Oh, okay then. One more won't harm the new image,' and he sat down and opened his paper once more.

SIX

It was to be two days before PC Crocker could begin his undercover surveillance of the guesthouse. He had received some superficial facial injuries after tumbling down the steps outside Clapham Police Station, and it was only after the visible swelling had gone down that he felt confident once again to dress up as his *alter ego*, Fleur. It was Friday evening when he first entered the vestibule of a large Victorian detached house, outside which was a discreet sign saying simply, 'Vacancies'.

The interior lighting was subdued, but Crocker could make out a rather grand staircase in front of him, while to the left an open door led into what appeared to be a small cocktail bar. As he wandered across the room, Crocker was surprised to see about half a dozen men in this female-only establishment, some sitting at low tables while others were standing about the room looking slightly uncomfortable. Crocker noted to himself that some of their faces seemed vaguely familiar. Behind the bar was a statuesque, elegantly dressed woman wearing a considerable quantity of gold jewellery. The professional crime-solver in Crocker, forever alert, noted as he moved towards her that this could be a possible motive for assault.

'May I speak to Ivy, please?' he said to the woman.

The woman looked at him, unsmiling. 'I'm Ivy. Who's asking?'

Crocker looked about him, aware of the proximity of others in the room. 'I've been sent by...' Crocker struggled. The men at the bar were within earshot and he did not want to blow his cover within the first five minutes of his mission. 'I was wondering if you had a spare room.' Crocker then winked in an obvious manner at Ivy, who simply looked at him in dismay. Realising that he had not made himself understood, he continued. 'I was sent by our mutual friend,' he said quietly and winked again.

Ivy peered at Crocker in the dim light of the small bar. 'You look a bit old,' she said. 'What's your specialty?'

Crocker believed he had been expected and was frustrated by this ongoing questioning. He looked around once more, leaned forward and whispered, 'My specialty is undercover work. I've brought my handcuffs.'

Ivy sighed. 'Well, we haven't had one of those for a while, I suppose. Wait over there with the other girls and I'll be along in a moment.'

Crocker walked through a set of open double doors into a large room, which was even less well-lit. Couches of various shapes and sizes lined the walls, above which hung paintings of women whom, Crocker noted, didn't seem to be wearing much in the way of clothing. Crocker was pleased to see the other residents of the guesthouse standing and chatting. He sidled up to one of them who was wearing a nurse's uniform. 'Just finished a late shift?' Crocker asked, smiling.

The girl looked at him with disdain. 'Who are you? Mary bloody Poppins?'

Crocker laughed good-naturedly at this bonhomie and turned his attention to a chambermaid who was obviously taking a break from her duties. 'Nice place,' he stated innocently.

'Yeah, it's all right. I've been in worse,' she observed. 'But since poor Rosie got it, we've been worried sick, 'aven't we, girls?'

'Ah,' thought Crocker to himself, 'not even in the place twenty minutes and already I'm on the trail.' Then, eager to build on this promising and unexpected opening, he said nonchalantly, 'Yes, I read about it. Poor Rosie. Has anyone been arrested?'

'Nah, but we know who done it, don't we, girls?' The other two nodded.

'Well, why don't you tell the police then?' Crocker looked at the three girls in turn, noticing that the third was also dressed unusually for Clapham, wearing a tight-fitting hooped blue and white shirt, a very short black leather skirt and a blue beret.

'They'd never believe us. But Ivy's got contacts in the police and a friend of hers is going to help, or so she says. Anyway, what are you doing here? You don't look like one of the usual girls.'

Crocker smiled. 'I do feel a bit frumpy compared to you three,' he admitted, adding, 'but that's just my disguise.' He winked at the nurse. 'Know what I mean?'

The girls just looked at him, puzzled. 'It's certainly different: but I suppose there are all sorts of weirdos out there. Good luck,' said the nurse. 'Well, I'd better get to work: do my first dressing of the night, so to speak.' So saying, she detached herself from the little group and wandered off to join one of the men in the bar. Crocker was impressed and made a mental note that the guesthouse had its own live-in nurse.

Suddenly, Ivy bustled up and took Crocker aside. She looked at him intently. 'Is your name Fleur?' she asked. 'You know, from the...' She looked about to make sure she was not being overheard. 'From the – *station.*'

Crocker smiled to himself. Clearly, Ivy had only just realised who he was. His disguise had been effective and his cover had not been blown. 'Yes, Madam. PC Crocker at your service,' and he lifted his wig and bowed slightly.

'Oh, for heaven's sake,' she replied. 'Quickly, come with me.'

Ivy led the way along a short corridor to a small office. Once inside, she sat down and smiled at Crocker. 'I'm sorry, but I didn't recognise you. Everyone's been so tense since Rosie was killed. Cecil said he'd send an undercover officer, but it didn't occur to me that it would be a PC in drag.' She sighed. 'Here, let me show you to your room.'

So Crocker was escorted up two flights of stairs to a small garret. As Ivy turned to leave, she said, 'If I were you, I would probably just stay in your room tonight and we'll chat about how we go about finding the killer tomorrow.'

'Well, I must say all this excitement has made me rather tired. I'll see you tomorrow first thing – say eight o'clock, for coffee?'

Ivy sighed. 'Make that twelve o'clock, and for gin. *Good night.*'

***

Andy had made an effort. He had bathed, washed his hair, shaved (with a new blade) and dressed himself in clean, if somewhat ill-fitting, clothes. He knew that Lucy couldn't drive, so by the simple process of borrowing a car from a friend, he had managed to persuade her that they should travel to the weekend house-party together. Thus, at six o'clock, dressed in unfashionably flared jeans, a flowery patterned shirt with a wide collar and Chelsea boots, he perched on his bar stool, which he had moved to the side of the room so that he could rest against the wall, lit a cigarette and opened a can of beer.

Eventually, Lucy entered the lounge, followed by a cloud of perfume. Having been at one of Rupert's house-parties before, she knew a little of the dress code, and instead of dressing as a go-go dancer, which she had done on the previous occasion, she had regaled herself in a more country style with a Barbour jacket, a heavy, knee-length russet skirt and sensible low-heeled shoes, while a woollen scarf adorned her neck. She walked past Andy and looked at herself in a mirror. 'I feel evva so frumpy dressed like this,' she said to herself as much as to Andy, who took a swig from his can. 'But last time I dressed really smart and I looked out of place.' Lucy turned away from the mirror. 'What do you think, Andy?'

Andy was thoughtful for a moment, trying to work out what the most appropriate answer would be. 'I think...' But he was interrupted before he could get any further.

'Don't answer that. I don't care. Remember, Andy, we are *not* going to this party as a couple. *All right*? And another thing – don't you embarrass me.' Lucy then turned to face Andy, and on seeing him her expression turned from surprise to amazement. 'It's not fancy dress, you know!'

Andy stubbed his cigarette out in the overflowing saucer that was the ashtray. 'What d'you mean?'

'I said it's not a fancy dress party.'

Confusion registered on Andy's otherwise vacuous face. 'I know.'

'Well, why are you dressed as Cliff Richard from about ten years ago, for God's sake?'

'I'm not.'

'Well, what are you dressed as?'

'Me!'

Lucy shook her head in dismay. 'Ugh. Let's go. Now, remember what I told you, Andy. Last time I went to Warren Hall, that twat Nigel mistook Lord Forsyth himself for the car park attendant. I've never been so embarrassed. Gave him a tip and everything, so show some respect for the man. Okay, Andy?'

'Yes, Lucy. Here, let me take your bags.'

Andy lifted Lucy's cases and led the way down the hall to the front door. Once outside, he stood back to allow Lucy to admire his borrowed car, an ancient Morris Minor Countryman.

'Ta-ra,' he sang, waving his arm at their transport.

Lucy simply stared at the car. 'Wot on earth is that?' she said, exasperated.

'That, Lucy, is a Morris Minor Countryman. A classic car ideally suited to a weekend in the country: hence its name – Countryman.'

'It's a heap of rubbish. The only thing holding it together is rust.' Lucy, who had clearly not yet entered into the party spirit, then added, 'It better not break down or you're a dead man, Andy Norris.'

Having stowed the luggage in the back, Andy revved the car into life and they set off for the shires, west of London.

SEVEN

It was to be several years before Andy was able to confide in anyone the events of the total disaster that was the weekend house-party at Warren Hall. Firstly, there was the little error of the car park attendant. Having dropped Lucy off at the front door of the elegant Georgian mansion, he drove the Morris Minor Countryman onto the gravel apron in front of the house, got out and started to retrieve the suitcases from the back of the car. Lucy, having ensured that she would not be sharing a room with Andy, immediately headed off to the main building. A man, wearing a flat cap and Wellington boots, then approached Andy. Remembering Lucy's earlier warning, Andy bowed deeply from the waist and said, 'Good evening, Your Lordship.'

The man seemed somewhat surprised by this greeting, but simply picked up the bags and said, 'Follow me.'

Andy, determined not to make the same inexcusable error that Nigel had made some years ago, replied, 'Oh no. Allow *me*, Your Lordship,' and started to wrestle the bags back.

The man, puzzled by this behavior, looked at Andy and said, 'Suit yourself then,' and led the way to the stable block where Lucy and Nigel had stayed three years before. Andy followed the man up a short steep staircase and into a small, somewhat spartan bedroom. The man showed Andy the bathroom and other facilities, then stood in front of him and coughed into the back of his hand. Andy was certainly not to make the same mistake that Nigel had made and tip His Lordship, so he bowed again and said, 'Thank you, Your Lordship.'

The man simply stood and looked at the ceiling, eventually dropping his gaze and coughing again. Andy's response was to bow once more and mutter, 'A great honour, Your Lordship.'

This charade continued for another thirty seconds before the man looked at Andy, muttered something about bloody pop singers being mean bastards, and stomped heavily down the stairs. Andy, pleased with how he had handled the situation so tactfully, then started to unpack his bag. A few minutes later, there came a knock on the door and in walked Rupert, his host.

'Andy, I'm so glad you could make it. Lucinda said that you might not be able to come.'

Andy shook Rupert's hand, remembering how Lucy had tried to hijack his invitation. 'Yes, but I've managed to rearrange things.'

'I'm so glad. I very much enjoyed our little pub-crawl in Clapham all those years ago and hoped to repay your hospitality. Anyway, I just wanted to pop in and welcome you.'

'Thanks, Rupert. That's kind. Your father was most helpful in showing me to my room.'

Rupert looked confused. 'Hardly likely, Andy. He died two years ago.' The sound that Andy made on hearing this cannot really be adequately described, but it was something between a squeal and a squeak. 'Come on over when you're ready,' Rupert continued. 'Informal dress this evening. By the way, you *will* be shooting tomorrow, won't you?' Rupert looked at Andy enquiringly. Andy, keen not to make another social gaffe, simply squeaked again.

'Oh, jolly good. That should make it a round dozen guns. See you later.' With that, Lord Rupert Forsyth, the 14th Earl, descended the steps of the stable block and strolled back to his mansion.

Andy could have cried. He had only been at Warren Hall less than an hour and had already made a complete prat of himself, not once but twice. He would have returned to London straight away if he hadn't promised to take Lucy back on Sunday. In retrospect, he appreciated that what he subsequently did was probably unwise – he reached for the bottle of whisky he had brought with him in case the party was a little light on alcoholic refreshment. You will remember that Andy was normally a lager drinker, and not a very good one at that, so the neat whisky burned his throat and made him cough. However, after a few swigs, he certainly felt more settled and was reasonably at ease with the world when he strolled across the yard and walked through the grand front doors of Warren Hall.

Once inside, however, his confidence evaporated like a wispy cloud on a summer's day. The house was bustling with elegant men and women and buzzing with animated conversation. Laughter echoed around the vast space as young and old alike chatted and joked confidently while sipping champagne from crystal glasses. Once again, Andy was about to turn and run when, from among one of the larger groups, a woman detached herself and approached him. 'Andrew, I'm so glad you could make it.' Lucinda, attired in an evening gown of considerable age, approached and kissed him on both cheeks while managing not to actually touch him at all. 'Oh, my dear,' she said, 'you're a breath of fresh air, and Lucy was right, you do look just like Cliff Richard. Now what you need is a drink.'

Lucinda took his hand firmly and virtually dragged Andy across the room to the old library which had been converted into a bar. 'Now, Peter,' Lucinda addressed the man serving drinks, 'I want you to get Andrew here anything he wants.' She turned to look at Andy. 'I think you drink beer, don't you? We ordered a barrel especially.' Andy looked at the man behind the bar and was horrified to see the car park attendant staring back at him. 'Now, Andrew, I must go and greet my other guests. Do enjoy yourself. I'll see you later.' And Lucinda was gone, leaving Andy facing Peter the barman, who smiled at him.

'Yes, sir,' said the car park attendant-cum-barman. 'What can I get you?'

Andy shuffled uneasily from foot to foot. 'A beer, please, if you have one?'

'I'll just check to see if we have any, sir.' His gaze then dropped to a barrel sitting on the table in front of him. 'Well, goodness me, I wonder what this could be. Bless my soul, it's a barrel.' Peter looked at Andy, a supercilious smile on his face. 'It's just possible that this might have beer in it. Let's see, shall we?'

He took a pint mug and turned the tap, from which issued brown liquid. Looking up, he said, 'Well, we are in luck, sir, aren't we?' and handed the filled mug to Andy.

Andy muttered quietly, 'Thank you,' took a deep draught of beer and, his confidence restored, wandered from room to room in search of Lucy.

Having failed to find her and knowing no one, he continued to wander aimlessly about, sometimes pretending that he was in a rush to speak to someone in another room, while at other times trying to give the impression that he was pleased to be standing alone with his own thoughts. With each circuit of the house, he had another pint. In later years he tried, without success, to calculate how many pints he had consumed that night. He never found out, but was informed that the barrel of ale was replaced mid-evening and that most of the other guests were drinking wine. Whatever the tally, by ten o'clock Andy was very relaxed indeed and enjoying himself considerably. In fact, he was so relaxed that he decided to sit down on one of the hard wooden benches that lined the long entrance hall. There he sat, pint in hand, trying to focus on those passing, occasionally offering them advice on whatever seemed to be appropriate.

The first inkling he had that all was not well was when he tried to stand up but failed. He knew he *could* stand, because he had been doing so earlier in the evening; indeed, he felt he had been pretty good at it. But now, each time he made an attempt to raise himself up from the seated position, nothing whatsoever happened. He looked at his legs, puzzled by their lack of effectiveness. After several more attempts, he managed to rise about a foot, only to immediately sit heavily back down on the bench. Eventually, summoning all his experience of similar encounters in the past, he struggled manfully to his feet and somehow managed to navigate his way back to his room, where he collapsed, still fully clothed, on to his bed.

Next morning, Andy was awakened by the first rays of dawn flooding through the uncurtained window. He closed his eyes again as the sunlight seemed to sear directly through his eye sockets into the very centre of his skull, where it bounced around various neurological structures, causing a series of painful electric shocks on the background of a deep throbbing sensation. He opened his eyes again and looked around the room where he had found himself, unsure as to where he was, until gradually the events of the previous night came back to him. His initial response was to panic. He remembered the embarrassment with the car park attendant, and then drinking a lot of beer. After that, his recollection of the evening grew somewhat vague, but he didn't remember being sick, and most importantly, he couldn't recall seeing Lucy all evening.

As he pondered on the events of the previous night, there came a knock at the door. 'Breakfast in ten minutes for the guns, Mr Norris.' Andy recognised the voice. It was the car park attendant-cum-barman and now valet.

The message was repeated. Could he detect a hint of amusement in the voice? 'Be right there,' Andy said with more confidence than he felt.

'Certainly, sir. I'll prepare your gun.'

Andy now remembered that he had agreed to go on the shoot. He sat on the side of his bunk and put his head in his hands. For the third time in less than twelve hours he considered driving straight back to London and for a third time he remembered he had promised to take Lucy back, and he couldn't let her down. More importantly, he remembered that the whole point of attending this nightmare of a weekend was to increase his standing in Lucy's eyes. 'Not an auspicious start, maybe,' he said to himself, 'but there's plenty of time to go.' He took a swig of whisky from his bottle. 'And things can only get better,' he thought – but he was wrong: they got worse, much worse.

EIGHT

PC Crocker normally slept soundly, but his slumber was severely disturbed during his first night in the guesthouse. The residents seemed to be having some sort of party and there were noisy comings and goings well into the early hours of the morning. Crocker presumed that the excitement was because it was Friday night: the end of the week, a time when the residents could let their hair down and maybe even have a drink or two. When he finally awoke the following morning, the house had fallen silent. By the time he had dressed carefully as his *alter ego*, Fleur, it was nearly ten o'clock and he was worried that he might have missed breakfast. His worst fears were realised when he went downstairs and discovered there was no sign of any activity whatsoever. As he expectantly entered the sitting room, where he presumed breakfast would be served, he was surprised to find the bar had not been cleared from the previous evening's revelries. Overflowing ashtrays and dirty glasses covered the table tops, and there was no evidence of the usual morning paraphernalia associated with his favourite meal of the day: no newspapers; no welcoming smell of freshly brewed coffee or salvers laden with bacon and eggs. Feeling hungry, he decided to dine elsewhere, so he let himself out and walked briskly to the Common, where he knew he could savour a full English breakfast at a very reasonable price. On one of the side streets just off the Common was a small café which he had often frequented when coming on or off duty. He was now becoming at one with his disguise, and by the time he entered the establishment he had completely forgotten that he was wearing women's clothing.

'Mornin', Ron,' he said breezily to the proprietor, as he rubbed his hands in gastronomic anticipation. 'Usual, please.'

Ron, a balding, slightly sweaty man who was wearing a rather grubby white T-shirt and apron, looked at Crocker in surprise. 'The *usual*, madam?'

'Yes, Ron, the...' Realising his error, Crocker attempted to cover his tracks. 'Oh, sorry,' he said, feigning surprise, 'I forgot. I thought I was in Fortnum and Mason's.' Then in his most refined tones he said, 'May I have a large cup of tea, a double portion of bacon and eggs with beans on the side.' He paused for a moment before adding, 'Yes, and some fried bread, please.'

Ron looked up at Crocker enquiringly. 'Do they serve that at Fortnum's?'

'Absolutely. In shovel loads, I can tell you. Heavy on the beans, please.'

Ron was puzzled. For good reasons, very few women ate in his café, and none came more than once: it was more of a male preserve. Yet here was a refined lady ordering a truck-driver's special. There was also something strangely familiar about this woman, but he couldn't quite fathom what.

'Sorry, miss, I must 'ave forgotten your name.'

'Mrs,' corrected Crocker.

'Sorry, Mrs, but I can't quite remember you. Is it a while since you've been in?'

'Yes, it has been a while. My name is Fleur. You may call me Fleur.'

'Ah yes, I remember,' lied the patron unconvincingly.

Crocker was now in full flow. 'Yes, I normally go to Fortnum's for breakfast, but this morning I became confused and mistook Clapham for Piccadilly.'

Ron frowned and simply said, 'Easily done.'

Crocker then smiled sweetly and wandered to a table, where he sat down, opened a newspaper and pretended to read in order to avoid attracting further attention.

After a hearty breakfast followed by a brisk walk around the Common, Crocker headed back to the guesthouse. By now it was nearly midday, but still the front door was closed and there was no sign of life. After letting himself in, he looked into the bar and there espied Ivy, sitting at one of the low tables, a cigarette in one hand, a large gin and tonic in a crystal tumbler in the other. She was looking a lot older than she had appeared the previous evening when Crocker had first met her, and she appeared to be wearing a pale pink dressing gown. As she lifted her eyes and registered Crocker's presence, she croaked, 'Oh, God! Not you,' and took a large gulp from her glass.

Crocker smiled engagingly. 'Morning, Ivy. Sleep well? Seemed to be quite a night last night?'

'Yes, you could say that,' she replied, before bursting into a fit of coughing.

Crocker was keen to proceed with his investigation, eager to start work. He recalled one of his favourite sayings, *Carpe diem*, and then frowned silently, unsure of its meaning. 'Well, Ivy, let's get started, shall we?'

'Oh, God,' uttered Ivy quietly, holding her head in her hands.

Crocker somehow instinctively sensed that this might not be the most appropriate time for his first interview of the investigation. 'Maybe you're feeling a bit under the weather? We could do it later?'

Ivy stubbed her cigarette out and emptied her glass. 'No, you're right, Fleur, or whoever you are, we should get on and try to find out who it is who killed Rosie Little.'

'Good. Now I think you said that you thought the murderer might be one of the men who work here?'

'No men work here,' replied Ivy, before realising her error. 'Well, of course men pop in from time to time, as indeed they did last night. You probably noticed one or two.' Ivy looked at Crocker and raised her eyebrows.

'Indeed I did,' replied Crocker. 'Workmen, I presume. Plumbers, electricians, that sort of thing?'

'Absolutely, Fleur. Spot on,' agreed Ivy.

'So you think it may be one of those tradesmen who did the dirty on our Rosie?'

'Yes, I think that may be so.'

'Any idea which one?'

'None at all, I'm afraid, but I think the girls...' – and Ivy hesitated – 'that is the residents, might have an idea, but they don't always confide in me. That's why it's so important that you stay undercover here and gain their confidence. They might be able to help, if they feel they can trust you.'

'Understood,' said Crocker firmly. 'I'll start right away. When would be convenient to interview them?'

'Difficult to say,' said Ivy, looking up at the ceiling. 'They usually come down mid-afternoon for something to eat. Probably best if you just wait here and have a surreptitious chat when they do appear.'

'Good idea, Ivy, that's exactly what I'll do,' said Crocker. 'The Chief wanted subterfuge, and subterfuge is what he'll get – in bucket loads.'

Ivy looked at Crocker, puzzled. 'The Chief?' Then she smiled. 'Ah yes, Cecil.'

'You know him?'

'In a kind of way, yes.'

'What kind of way?'

'Oh, business, Fleur, business.'

'Yes, of course. Well, the Chief wants me to solve this case so the residents of this fine guesthouse can once again be free: free of fear, free to come and go without having to worry about the possibility of molestation or attack.'

'Excellent, Fleur; that would be really excellent. Now, if you'll excuse me I have some jobs to do.' Ivy hesitated. 'Book plumbers and things like that. Never ending, Fleur, never ending – the work involved running a guesthouse.' So saying, she disappeared through the door of the bar in the direction of her little office.

Crocker decided that as each of the residents came down he would casually engage them in conversation and subtly bring up the topic of the murder.

He had to wait nearly an hour before the first resident entered the bar. Crocker recognised her as the nurse he had met the previous night and noted that she was not in uniform. In fact, she seemed to be dressed in her pyjamas and was yawning and stretching. 'Probably her day off,' thought Crocker to himself. The wait had obviously dulled Crocker's normally astute cerebration, because as soon as he had attracted her attention he said, 'Well, no murders last night then. That's good, isn't it?'

Upon hearing this, the nurse simply burst into torrents of tears. Crocker, realising that this may not have been the most subtle of approaches, went over to put an arm around her shoulder in a manly, comforting fashion. Once again he forgot that he was now in character and was quite taken aback when the nurse suddenly flung her arms around his neck and began to sob violently. Between spasms, and still clinging to Crocker's neck, she managed to blurt out, 'Fleur, oh, Fleur. Poor Rosie. Who would have believed it?'

Crocker, his razor-sharp intellect now fully restored, immediately realised that this was an investigative opportunity. Although somewhat uneasy in the role of comforter, he managed to console the nurse. 'There, there,' he murmured several times until the sobbing grew less. 'Have you any idea who might have wanted to kill Rosie?' asked Crocker innocently. This precipitated a further spasm of sobbing, interrupted only by vigorous eye-rubbing with a dirty linen handkerchief, thereby spreading eye-shadow liberally across the upper half of her face.

'It's one of the clients, I'm sure. But none of us knows which one.' The un-uniformed nurse began to sob again.

'You mean the tradesmen?' said a confused Crocker.

'You can call them what you like, dear.'

'Maybe one took a liking to Rosie and when she turned him down he killed her.' Crocker was pleased with this little theory which he had worked out while they had been talking, but all it did was to precipitate another bout of sobbing. 'There, there,' Crocker continued soothingly for several minutes until the girl once more calmed down.

Then she managed to say, 'Maybe. Certainly quite a few of the men took a shine to Rosie. She was very pretty and younger than me.'

'Yes, but you've probably got more qualifications,' said Crocker encouragingly. 'They take time and study.'

'Qualifications?' The nurse once more looked puzzled. 'Well, yes, I suppose I do have some talents which take a while to learn.'

'Come, come, my dear, you are far too modest.'

The nurse smiled. 'You're so nice, Fleur. Whatever got *you* into this business?'

Crocker was about to say, 'A desire to keep the streets of Clapham safe, to rid them of footpads and pickpockets,' when he remembered just in time that he was undercover. 'Oh, I'm just trying to earn a crust – to keep body and soul together.'

'Aren't we all?' The nurse then looked at Crocker and smiled. 'Thanks for the chat, Fleur. I feel better for it, but I'd better go and get dressed now.'

'Are you on duty tonight, as well?'

'Yes. I work every night. Sometimes I have Thursdays off and go to the cinema or something like that.'

Crocker looked at her with tenderness. 'Long hours. But that's dedication, isn't it?'

Once again the nurse frowned. 'Well, I guess you could put it that way. Anyway, I'm off to put my uniform on.'

As the girl left to get ready for what Crocker presumed was another late shift, he sat down at one of the tables in the bar to review what he had learned so far. It seemed likely that Rosie's killer was one of the tradesmen who did odd jobs at the guesthouse and that he was still working here, as there had been no reports of jobs left undone or tradesmen not turning up for work. All he had to do was wait around and observe the tradesmen when they came, which appeared to be in the evenings. 'Probably overtime – cash in hand,' thought Crocker. Maybe he could engage them in conversation and trick the guilty party into giving himself away.

The chambermaid then entered the bar. Interestingly, she, too, had not yet had time to put on her uniform and was wearing a dressing gown and fluffy slippers.

'Mornin',' she said on seeing Fleur. 'You're dressed early.'

'Early bird catches the worm, or so they say,' replied Crocker.

'Not this early, dear. Pour me a gin, would you?'

Crocker was surprised by this request, but, professional to the last, did as he was asked. Once again he took the opportunity to discuss Rosie's murder. Shortly afterwards, the French girl arrived. Surprisingly, she, too, was still in her nightgown, and her French accent, so thick the night before, had all but vanished.

Later that day, as Crocker reviewed his afternoon's work, he concluded that all the residents of the guesthouse seemed to agree that one of the tradesmen was likely to be the killer, but none knew which one. They also seemed to think it was likely that he would be one of the men who would be attending for work that evening, and all of them were worried sick that the murderer might take a shine to them and that they might be the next victim.

NINE

Bernard Ponsonby-Titchmarsh was the Conservative councillor for Clapham Common, and he was tired. He had been on the council for over twenty years and wanted to retire. Twenty years of sitting through council meetings had not only gradually eroded his zeal and enthusiasm for the job, but had also given him painful haemorrhoids. He had repeatedly offered his resignation to his party leader, only to be told that he could not resign or retire because in the resulting by-election the Conservatives would almost certainly lose the seat, thereby losing their majority on the council. The Tory councillor had even thought of trying to get himself disqualified, but he wasn't sure quite how to go about it. He was too old to have an affair with his secretary, and wasn't at all sure if she would co-operate even if he were up to it, and he had no predilection for any sexual deviancy, which had been the downfall of so many of his colleagues. The other popular way to get expelled, it seemed to him, was to take drugs, misappropriate public money or be otherwise fraudulent in some way. He had been taking drugs for years, mainly for gout, but that didn't seem to meet the criteria for expulsion; and try as he might to own up to fictitious fraud, no one took him seriously. The previous year he had admitted to the Leader of the Council that he'd fraudulently claimed for tea and biscuits on his expenses, not once, but several times. The leader had simply laughed and said, 'Is that all?'

So Bernard Ponsonby-Titchmarsh simply hung on, waiting for the next council elections, when he would be able to stand down. That, however, would not be for another three years, so it was with increasing desperation that he continued to attend council meetings and place his rubber ring on his customary seat as far away from the action as possible, where he could read his newspaper and quietly doze until the end of the session.

He had no idea how he had come to be invited to Lord Forsyth's house-party, but thought that a weekend away might make a change and maybe even give him an opportunity to perform some heinous indiscretion that would result in his disqualification. The other deciding factor was that one of his few pleasures in life was shooting, and so that was how he found himself, that Saturday morning, cradling a twelve-bore and strolling some way behind the main group of guns who were excitedly pushing on ahead. He knew from past experience that the shoot would involve several hours of walking, along with sitting for prolonged periods on cold, hard surfaces, all of which were destined to exacerbate his haemorrhoidal problem. Hence, first thing that morning, he had taken the precaution of carefully wrapping a large towel, in a nappy-like fashion, around his buttocks and placing a large sheet of cardboard down the back of his trousers. Thus attired, he could sit down with only a modicum of discomfort. Little did he know that this preparation was not only going to save his life, but would also allow him to resign his seat (that is the one on the council) once and for all.

Andy, you will remember, never had any intention of going on the shoot, but had not been at his most mentally alert first thing that morning when Peter, manservant-cum-barman-cum-armourer, had asked him whether he would be taking part. Without conscious thought he had said he would be along, when what he'd meant to say was that he would like to stay in bed all day. Thus it was that Andy found himself in the main hallway of Warren Hall, inappropriately dressed like Cliff Richard, amongst a mêlée of excited men of all ages who were wearing wax jackets, Wellington boots and peaked caps. When they were not laughing or chatting, they were peering down the barrels of shotguns and filling their pockets with cartridges. The nearest thing to a wildfowl shoot that Andy had been on was when a travelling fair came to Clapham Common and he won a cuddly toy for shooting a glass bottle with a .22 rifle. As he stood self-consciously in the draughty hallway, he realised that, once again, he had managed to get himself into a predicament which seemed destined to end unfavourably for him. He also knew that the only way to extricate himself would be to do the honourable thing: admit that he was a complete fraud, had never handled a gun before, let alone been on a shoot, that he had a hangover and simply wanted to go back to bed. While getting dressed he had prepared a little speech which he felt would excuse him from the shoot without losing face completely. He decided that he would endeavour to take his host to one side and explain that he disapproved in principle of shooting defenceless animals, or birds – or whatever it was they were going to kill that day – and could not take part for ethical reasons. He thought this would place him on the moral high ground and leave him with a modicum of credibility. He would then ask Rupert politely if he would mind awfully if he went back to bed.

After a while, Andy espied Rupert and began to make his way through the crowd towards him, when two things happened simultaneously. Peter, the valet-cum-barman-cum-car park attendant-cum-armourer, approached him brandishing a twelve-bore shotgun and said, 'Mr Norris, this gun should be fine for you,' offering it to him with a rather supercilious smile; at exactly the same moment as Andy glimpsed Lucy descending the rather grand stairway heading towards the dining room.

Thus it was that, instead of delivering his speech pronouncing his disapproval of shooting, Andy said, 'Thank you, Peter,' took the gun and looked down the barrel as he had observed the others doing, while trying to look as much like Clint Eastwood, whom Lucy adored, as possible.

That was how Andy found himself at the back of the duck shoot, trudging across a misty field towards a lake where they hoped to find some wildfowl. Andy, overweight and unfit, quickly fell behind the rest of the shoot to find himself about twenty yards behind an elderly-looking gentleman who seemed to have a disproportionately large backside.

What happened next was a complex series of events which could never have been predicted and was the outcome of several unrelated events in Andy's recent past. The first was the fact that he was still nervous of loud noises. Ever since the attempted assassination on his person, he would be startled by unexpected bangs. A car backfiring would make him jump over the nearest wall and hide, while a slamming door would cause him to run for cover. The second factor was that Andy had no knowledge whatsoever of guns. When Peter had handed the gun to him it had been properly broken to make it safe, but as soon as he had accepted it he had inserted a cartridge into the breech, clicked the barrel into place and pointed it in the direction of the ceiling in the way he had seen Clint Eastwood do in *Hang 'em High*. All of this charade was in case Lucy happened to be watching, and Andy, against all the odds, was still out to impress. It was a combination of these factors that resulted in Andy murdering the council member for Clapham Common, for it was he who was walking just a few yards ahead of him. Well, Andy didn't actually murder him, but attempted to. Way ahead of the two of them, near the lakeside, one of the leaders of the shoot decided to take a potshot at some low-flying geese, and it was the resulting noise that startled Andy. His arm shot up, his finger slipped on to the trigger and the gun exploded, discharging a considerable amount of lead shot directly into Bernard Ponsonby-Titchmarsh's backside.

To the councillor for Clapham Common, the discharge felt rather as though someone had kicked him in the rear. Wondering what had happened and surprised by the noise, he placed his hand on his backside and realised that his trousers had been blown off and that the piece of cardboard covering his posterior was now full of little holes. Confused, he turned round to see a youngish-looking man with a striking resemblance to an overweight Cliff Richard, looking with a mixture of surprise and bewilderment at the end of the barrel of his gun, from which a plume of smoke was issuing.

The next few hours were a blur for Andy. He remembered helping the old gentleman back to the mansion, an ambulance being called, and then, while apologising profusely, gently helping to remove the smouldering remains of what was left of the man's trousers and what appeared to be a charred towel tied around the man's buttocks.

It was only after trouser and towel remnants and all pieces of cardboard had been removed that a full damage assessment could be performed. To everyone's amazement, the councillor for Clapham Common's bottom had hardly been damaged and that the effects of the shooting were limited to one or two patches of reddened skin. The councillor's life had been saved by his piles.

Andy was bereft and continued to apologise. Bernard Ponsonby-Titchmarsh, his posterior now wrapped in a blanket, simply smiled as the ambulance men carried him away on a stretcher and said, 'Mr Norris, please don't apologise: you have really done me a great favour.' He then waved a friendly farewell to the little group of guests that had gathered to see him off.

Once the ambulance had left, Andy sat down in the now vacated vestibule to reflect on the events of the day thus far. A few moments later, he heard footsteps and looked up to see Lucy approaching him. To say her expression was stern would be a grossly inadequate description of her demeanour – somewhat akin to describing a pack of rabid dogs as just being friendly.

Andy, never at his best when under pressure, looked up and said, 'Hello, Lucy, how's your day going so far?'

Lucy knew that there were no words adequate to the occasion and that only direct action would suffice, so she walked up to Andy and kicked him as hard as she could in the genitals.

Andy doubled up with pain, grasped his groin and started to remonstrate. He only got as far as, 'But, Lucy, it was an accident—' before he saw Lucy start her run-up for a second attack. It was Lucinda, however, who saved Andy from further assault.

'Andrew, well done on shooting that boring old fart. It's a pity you didn't kill him, but I suppose you weren't to know that he would be wearing a bulletproof nappy.' Lucinda turned her gaze to Lucy, 'You know, Lucy dear, these parties are so much more entertaining now that you and Andrew come along. They used to be terminally boring; nothing ever happened – but now you never know who's going to be killed next. You're a breath of fresh air, both of you.' Lucinda looked down at Andy, who was valiantly attempting to stand up. 'Well, I don't know about you two, but I'm ready for a drink. All this excitement has given me a thirst – do come along.'

Lucy reluctantly ceased her assault and turned to follow Lucinda, while Andy warily followed behind. Peter, now once more a barman, jokingly held his hands high as Andy approached, laughingly saying, 'Don't shoot, it's a fair cop.'

The events of the morning had adversely affected both Lucy's and Andy's sense of humour, and neither saw the funny side of this quip, but Her Ladyship smiled and said sweetly, 'He's such a card. Aren't you, Peter? Now stop messing about. We need drinks – large ones, and quickly.'

'Yes, Your Ladyship,' replied the chastened valet-cum-barman-cum-comedian.

Andy wanted desperately to return to London, while Lucy desperately wanted him to do just that, but their hosts would have none of it, and so Andy and Lucy had to spend the rest of the weekend trying to avoid each other. Andy did have one last attempt to break the ice with Lucy, but only got as far as, 'Lucy, I wonder—' before her raised foot plainly indicated to him that reconciliation was unlikely in the foreseeable future, if ever.

The drive back to London the following day was painful. Not a word was spoken the whole journey. On their arrival back at Parkview, Lucy slammed the car door, causing one of the wing mirrors to fall off, then stormed into the house and fled upstairs to her bedroom.

Andy, alone once again, tried to make some sense of the events of the weekend. Desperate to sit down and relax, he looked longingly at where the settee used to be, then sighed, opened a can of beer and lit a cigarette. He tried to sit on the bar stool, but his testicles were too sore, so he sat on the floor and turned on the television as the news was just beginning. As Andy gazed at the screen, he was startled to see peering out at him the familiar features of Bernard Ponsonby-Titchmarsh explaining to a reporter that, following a shooting accident, it was with great regret that he had resigned as councillor for Clapham Common. He went on to state that because of that tragic accident, he would be unable to sit through council meetings, or indeed sit down at all, for a considerable period of time, and therefore felt it was only appropriate that he should stand down as the local councillor, being unable to fulfil the responsibilities required of him.

TEN

'What is wrong with you, man? Why is it you went on a killing spree?' Zephaniah was seated on the opposite side of the Herald Lounge Bar to Andy and his voice was growing louder and louder until he was shouting across the room at his friend. 'You said you was goin' to try to get off with that Lucy bird, not assassinate half the Greater London Council. You is a liability, man. A liability – that's what you is.' Zephaniah wagged his finger in Andy's direction, his eyes now wide. 'You stay away from me, d'you hear? Is you armed?'

Andy just sighed. 'For heaven's sake, Zeph, it was an accident.'

'So was that tramp wot was killed because he sat down next to you. You're a liability. People just die if they is anywhere near to you, man. Are you going to shoot up this pub? Maybe if you don' like the beer, you just kill the barman?'

'Calm down, Zeph.'

'Calm down? How can I be calm when I'm sitting next to a mass murderer? A man who might kill you as soon as look at you. You is dangerous, man.'

'For heaven's sake, it was just an accident; and anyway, no one was killed.'

'That's what you say, but I don' know no more. This could jus' be the tip of the iceberg. Know wot ah mean?'

'I just accidentally shot a man in the bum, that's all. He's not dead, and, in fact, I did him a favour.'

Zephaniah's eyes widened in dismay. 'If that's doing a favour, man, I don' want to be around when you is really trying to upset someone. Here, get me a rum and Coke and put some music on before you kill anyone else.'

Andy Norris wearily got to his feet. It was the week after the little unpleasantness at Warren Hall. Lucy still wasn't talking to him, and this was the third tirade of the week from Zephaniah that he'd been at the receiving end of. Andy tried to change the subject. 'At least we won the Eurovision Song Contest, Zeph. That's good, isn't it?'

'Don' try to change the subjec', man; jus' get them drinks.' Soon, the Brotherhood of Man were singing 'Save Your Kisses For Me' and Andy settled down with a fresh pint and a cigarette.

Zephaniah took a sip of his rum and Coke. 'Hey, man, you see that the Minister for Drought has a new job?'

'Is that right?"

'Yeah. He's now Minister for Floods.' Zephaniah was referring to the rapid change in the weather, from the hottest summer for years to unprecedented rainfall. Zephaniah then put his paper down on the table in front of him, looked at the ceiling thoughtfully for a moment and then addressed Andy from where he was sitting at the other side of the room. 'Hey, man, now's your chance.'

'What d'you mean, now's my chance?'

'You know you is always goin' on about being able to run the country better than them Muppets who are at present. Well, now's your chance.'

'What d'you mean? Now's my chance?'

'There's goin' to be one of them council by-elections. An' all because you shot the sitting member.'

'Sadly, he's not going to be doing too much sitting for a while,' observed Andy with a smile.

'Well, man, don' you geddit? *You* could stand. You said all you needed was a vacancy and you would put yourself forward. Now's your chance.'

Andy was thoughtful. 'I'm not sure if the person who shot the outgoing councillor would be allowed to stand.'

'No reason why not. You said you did him a favour. Although personally I think anyone who needs someone to shoot them, as a favour, suggests that they don't get out enough or are soft in the head.'

'I'm not sure, Zeph.'

'You see, that's you all over. You is all talk. You say something, then when the opportunity come along, you bottle it. You're scared. You're scared that someone might shoot you up the backside. You can dish it out, man, but you can't take it. That's your problem.' Zephaniah picked up his paper in disgust.

'I'm not scared, Zeph. I'm just not sure if it's the right time for me. I've got my career to think about.'

'And wot career might that be?'

'Well, I suppose I *am* in a bit of a dead-end job.'

***

Students of politics will recall the process of electing a member of council when there is a by-election. Anyone of good standing can become a candidate if they pay a deposit, complete a set of nomination papers and submit them to the Returning Officer in the knowledge that they will get the deposit back if they poll over five percent of the vote. The reader will also recall that no candidate may withdraw after the close of nominations. The summer of 1977 was a turbulent time in politics, with a strong Conservative government, the Labour Party in disarray and a weak Liberal Party, which would soon become an SDP-Liberal alliance, the precursor of the Liberal Democrats.

'So, let me get this straight, Andy. We're going to be the Beer and Darts Party?' The landlord of the Nellie in Clapham looked at Andy quizzically.

'Yeah. That's right, Ted. I'll be the candidate; Zeph from the Herald Lounge Bar has agreed to be my agent; and we thought it would be nice if you would be chairman, as you run a business in the constituency, or ward, or whatever they call it.'

Andy had decided to run for council on a BAD Party ticket. Since the resignation of Bernard Ponsonby-Titchmarsh, and the events surrounding it, there had been considerable media interest in the contest and the race was now keenly contested. As expected, there was a Tory, a Labour and a Liberal nomination for what was a marginal seat. Then there was the token loony, who on this occasion was a skinny man representing the Martian Party, and finally there was Andy himself.

The reason Andy had eventually given in to Zephaniah's bullying and thrown his hat into the ring was that he thought it might, just might, demonstrate to Lucy that he was a man with a future: a man of ambition, someone to be taken seriously, a man with *gravitas*; not just an unlucky fat bastard who managed to shoot people accidentally in the backside, but a person of integrity and substance. He also considered that, as there wasn't a hope in hell of him winning, there was nothing to lose. He could bask in the attention that would follow from his candidacy, his own brief moment in the spotlight, attempt once more to seduce Lucy, then return to his ambition-free existence as soon as the polls closed.

So Andy paid his deposit, registered The Beer and Darts Party, submitted a set of nomination papers and was duly declared validly nominated. For his trouble and a considerable amount of money, he was given a free copy of the electoral register and informed that he had free use of public rooms for meetings as long as he paid for lighting and heating. He had yet to have a full meeting of the whole party: that is, all three of them, because of competing commitments, but he had ongoing policy discussions with Zephaniah on an almost nightly basis in the Herald Lounge Bar, and with Ted, the chairman, most weekends when there was a home darts match.

It was during a lull in one such match that Andy managed to have a strategy meeting with his chairman. 'What do you think should be in our manifesto, Ted?' he asked.

Ted thought for a moment. 'How about reducing the tax on beer?'

'Good one, Ted, that's brilliant. Hey, what about fags as well?'

'Yes, that'll attract the floating voters.'

'And the smoking voters. What about our foreign policy?'

'We don't want none of them.'

'What d'you mean, we don't want none of them?'

'We don't want no foreigners,' answered Ted, surprised that Andy hadn't followed his political reasoning.

'Okay. What's our policy on nuclear weapons?'

Ted was thoughtful and continued to dry a pint glass with a dirty tea towel. 'Difficult one.' Suddenly, he put the towel down. 'I know! We could sell them to pay for a reduced tax on booze and fags.'

'Brilliant, Ted, you're a natural. I think that just about wraps it up. I don't know why politicians make such a fuss about manifestos and policies. We've managed to draw this up during a break in a darts match.'

'What was Zeph's contribution?'

'He's worried about inflation.'

'What does he want to do about it?'

'He's going to make it illegal.'

Ted looked puzzled. 'I wonder why no one else has thought of that?' he replied, impressed with the simplicity of the concept.

'He also wants to increase the number of wives we can have at any one time.'

'Fine. That shouldn't be controversial.'

'Right, Ted, I'll type up the manifesto after work tomorrow and then we'll have to attend the hustings.'

'What are they?'

'No idea, mate. Excuse me, it's my throw.'

***

Clapham Common was a marginal seat and there could be no guarantee that another Conservative candidate would be returned. Justin Parker, their candidate, at forty-eight, had come to politics late after a successful career in commerce. He was a wealthy man and had been a substantial donor to the party on the understanding that when a seat became vacant he would be allowed to contest it. His personal statement outlining why the worthy population of Clapham Common should vote for him consisted of the fact that he had been to Rugby School, was an ex-officer in the Irish Guards and had made lots of money in the City. The more astute political observer might have wished for his policies to be fleshed out just a trifle more, but to Justin, policy issues were a mere irrelevance. As far as he was concerned, the *status quo* was the holy grail of politics, to be maintained at all costs, and he could ensure this by meeting like-minded colleagues in several of London's most prestigious clubs.

The Labour candidate had only recently discovered that women were now allowed to vote, and found the information disquieting. His appeal had always been to the working-man. Bill Bishop, or BB to his friends, was a hard man. 'Hard but fair' he liked to say about himself. A person of considerable bulk, here was a man who wanted his tea on the table at six o'clock, and woe betide anyone in the vicinity if it wasn't. This was a man, a Yorkshireman no less, who could eat peas with a knife and often did; someone who was not afraid to kick a dog or tug the ears of small children affectionately until they cried. Bill knew he had a wife, as it was she who cooked his tea every day, but he had long ago forgotten her name. Yes, dear reader, if I have given the impression that this was a typical, old-fashioned Labour politician,

I have succeeded in my task; not, you understand, that I am one for political stereotypes. BB was a traditional Labour candidate, not one of those poncy, lefty, free-thinking, can't-make-a-decision types that we see in the party these days. As for the Liberal candidate, well, there is really nothing worth saying, as is usually the case about members of that particular party. No one ever saw the Martian candidate, as he was always communing with his colleagues in outer space. Some questioned his very existence, but he had paid his deposit, submitted his nomination papers, and therefore was as entitled to his moment in the limelight along with free use of public rooms as long as he paid for heating and lighting, as did the other candidates.

It was clearly a two-horse race between Conservative and Labour, and it was neck and neck. That is why both Justin Parker and Bill Bishop tried to improve the odds in their favour.

ELEVEN

'Cecil, now I'm not goin' to beat about the bush. I need your 'elp.' Bill Bishop was not a man to pussy-foot about when it came to doing business, even if it *was* with the Chief Superintendent of Police for Clapham. 'Now, *you* know and *I* know that we 'ave mutual friends, which we probably best keep quiet about.' BB tapped the side of his nose. 'Know what I mean?' The Chief Super simply coughed into the back of his hand and swivelled from side to side in his chair. 'Now, I'm a plain-spoken man, Cecil, and the thing is, I'm standing for the Council in this 'ere by-election.'

The Chief Super, who was beginning to feel a trifle sick from all his swivelling, brought his chair to a standstill. 'Ah!' was all he said, without looking up from his desk.

'Yes, I want to be the next councillor for Clapham Common, and the only person standing in my way is that posh Conservative bastard, Justin Parker, who's just ahead in the polls. But...,' and here Bill Bishop leant forward and looked the Chief Super directly in the eye, 'it's neck and neck, believe you me. It's as close as it can be, so I need a spot of 'elp.'

BB sat back in his chair. The Chief looked at him and said, 'Ah!'

'I'd make it worth your while if I'm elected, I can tell you. 'Ow does Chief Constable sound, Cecil, eh?'

'Ah!'

'Or maybe even – *Sir* Cecil?'

As you may have gathered, up until this point the Chief Super was having difficulty articulating himself, but now he found the words to suit the moment and said, 'Ah,' once more, but on this occasion the intonation said it all – in barrel loads. 'Ahh,' he repeated.

'Yes, all I need is a bit of muck raked up on the posh bastard. Something accidentally leaked to the press. You know – maybe something to do with extra-marital sex, preferably with a boy or an underage girl. That sort of thing. Know wot I mean?'

The Chief Super coughed and said, 'Ah.'

'Well, I can see you're busy, Cecil, so I'll be off; but remember, a little something that might discredit our true blue friend in the *Evening News* would be very much appreciated.' BB leant forward once more to emphasise his point. 'If *not*, well, there may be a little something else that leaks, know wot I mean?' BB looked at his watch. 'Well, it's nearly teatime. I'll let myself out, Cecil.' BB smiled at the Chief Super: well, he turned the ends of his lips upwards, but it came out more as a grimace than a smile.

'Ah,' said the Chief, and started to swivel agitatedly once more as the door closed behind the Labour candidate.

***

Justin was equally concerned. He knew that his slender lead could disappear overnight and felt that his campaign needed revitalising. He knew that the normal voting classes would have already made their minds up and would vote along traditional party lines, but there was a great underworld of chronic non-voters out there who, if they could be persuaded to vote for him, might swing the balance in his favour. Justin Parker needed someone to reach parts of the electorate that no one else could, and he knew the best person for the job, the ideal campaign manager, and that person was a man called Crusher Ericsson. Crusher wasn't Ericsson's real given name – he hadn't used that since he was a child, when he'd discovered that it made everyone laugh. No one knew why he had acquired the epithet Crusher, but, at well over six feet tall, built like a gorilla with biceps the girth of tree trunks and hands the size of dinner plates, Justin wondered if it might just have something to do with his physique.

That evening, Justin turned up the collar of his overcoat and walked up the short path to the guesthouse where he knew Crusher would be spending the evening. Sure enough, he was at the bar, talking to a strange-looking, middle-aged spinsterish lady. He crossed the room to the bar and tapped the big man on the shoulder. Crusher didn't like having his shoulder tapped and swung round, his fist raised in anger, ready to thump his assailant.

'Whoah, whoah,' cried Justin as he jumped back and held both arms up in a gesture of surrender. 'It's me.'

Crusher, recognising Justin from previous political campaigns, said, 'Oh, it's you,' and dropped his fist to his side.

'Yes, Crusher. I'm in need of your skills. I want you to do some canvassing for me.'

Crusher looked at the middle-aged lady standing next to him and said to her, 'I'm sorry about this, but I need to do some business. Don't go away, I'll be back in a moment.' Crusher then led Justin to a table in the corner of the room, where they both sat down. 'So, Mr Politician, how may I be of assistance?'

'Keep your voice down, Crusher,' said Justin, looking about the room surreptitiously to ascertain if anyone was listening. No one appeared to be paying the least attention to them, apart from the odd-looking lady at the bar who was gazing uninterestedly in their general direction. 'I need you to do some campaigning on my behalf,' he continued.

'What does that involve?'

'Canvassing. Knocking on faces... I mean doors. Telling people that I'm the best candidate. Persuading the floating voters that they might be best voting for me or...' – Justin lowered his voice to a whisper – 'they might just end up floating themselves. Know what I mean?'

'What's in it for me?'

'Well, Crusher, just imagine how useful it would be for you to know the person who is the councillor for your patch.' Justin looked at the big man knowingly.

Crusher was quiet for a moment. 'I'd love to, but I'm just about to go on holiday.' Crusher made as though to get up.

'Plus a grand,' said Justin quietly.

Crusher stood still and hesitated. 'Thing is, I was really looking forward to my holiday. I've been a bit run down lately. Then there's all them cancellation fees and things.'

'Okay, Crusher, fifteen hundred, and that's my final offer.'

'Done.' Crusher didn't shake hands, but simply strolled back to the bar, where he once again engaged in conversation with the rather frumpy woman.

Seeing that Justin was now alone, the nurse began to sidle over to him, but before she was halfway across the room he stood up and disappeared rapidly into the Clapham night.

At the bar, PC Crocker, or rather Fleur – for it was he who had been chatting to Crusher – thought that he recognised the man who had been talking quietly with the big man.

'Who was that, Crusher?' he asked when he returned.

'Sorry, can't tell you, Fleur. Classified.' Crusher hesitated as though lost for words. 'Fleur,' he said after a moment, 'it's been really nice to meet you tonight. I'd like to stay, but I've just accepted a job and will need to get on with it straightaway.'

'Emergency, is it?'

'You could say that, but what I want to say, Fleur, is that you're different to the other girls and I'd like to see you again.'

Crocker, who had just taken a gulp of beer, coughed and spluttered. 'Oh, good,' he said, wiping his mouth with the back of his hand.

'I best be off, but I'll be in next week and I'd like another little chat with you, Fleur.' Crusher then reached into his trouser pocket and took out a sheaf of bank notes, from which he peeled one off and gave it to Crocker. 'Here you are, Fleur, here's twenty pounds. Have a drink on me and look after yourself until next week, okay?' Crocker hesitated momentarily. 'Here, take it,' said Crusher in a tone that did not encourage refusal. Speechless, Crocker took the note and then froze as his benefactor kissed him on the cheek, before walking purposefully out of the bar and following Justin into the Clapham night.

It had been a confusing evening for Crocker. A few hours earlier, as had been previously agreed, he had met up with the other residents. The nurse was now on duty again – ready for any emergency, no doubt – while the chambermaid was once more dressed in her work clothes, and the French girl was looking and sounding more Gallic than ever. As Crocker had expected, a number of tradesmen drifted in during the evening and were taken by one of the residents to be shown the various domestic problems that needed fixing. After half an hour or so, the job presumably done, they would return to the bar, have a drink and then leave.

Mid-evening, the door had banged open and a huge gorilla of a man entered the bar. Suddenly, the atmosphere in the room, which until then had been quite relaxed – even jovial – became tense. The residents seemed to almost physically shrink in an attempt to hide in the darkness of its recesses.

'Evening, Crusher,' said Ivy, attempting a smile.

'Usual,' was all the giant said. Ivy nervously poured a beer and handed it over to the man, who took a sip and looked around the room. Crocker was at the other end of the bar and, on seeing him, the big man smiled and approached. 'You're new here,' he said.

Taken aback, Crocker replied, 'Just staying for a few days. Business, *you* know.'

'Yeah, I know. What's your name?'

Crocker's voice trembled as he replied. 'Fleur.'

'Fleur?' Crusher took another sip of beer. 'Nice name. What can I get you to drink, Fleur?'

Without thinking, Crocker replied, 'Oh, a pint, please,' and as soon as the words had been uttered he knew he had made a bad mistake. However, Crusher simply smiled.

'You're my kind of girl, Fleur.' He turned to the barmaid. 'Ivy, a pint for Fleur and another for me.'

Ivy was worried, very worried. She knew Crusher had a foul temper and was easily roused; and she could only imagine what might happen when he discovered that Fleur was not only a police officer, but a male one at that. As she passed over the beers, her hands were shaking. Crocker, now equally nervous, took a long draft of beer, emptying half his glass in one gulp. Crusher smiled and followed suit. 'Yeah, you're my kind of girl all right.' He turned to Ivy. 'Where 'ave you been hiding this one, Ivy?' he asked without taking his eyes off Crocker.

'Only been here a couple of days,' replied Ivy nervously.

It was then that the prospective Conservative councillor entered the room and tapped Crusher Ericsson on the shoulder, thereby almost certainly saving Crocker from what could only have developed into a truly tricky situation.

TWELVE

'I'll be out tonight.' Andy said this without looking up from his copy of the *Evening News*. He was perched on the bar stool, which Lucy had placed once more in the centre of the lounge at Parkview in order to make sitting as uncomfortable as possible for him. Andy had not detected any sign of a thaw in the relationship between him and Lucy: any communication between them being restricted to matters of an essential nature and conducted in monosyllables. Lucy, basking in her friendship with Lady Forsyth, had been concerned that the shooting, albeit accidental, of a local councillor by her housemate might have an adverse effect on their relationship. However, she needn't have worried, as both Lucinda and her new husband considered the incident to be the highlight of what had otherwise been a singularly unexciting weekend.

Andy, perched on his stool, knew that Lucy was in the kitchen and within earshot. He needed to attract her attention so that he could subtly, almost accidentally, inform her that he was now a man with prospects: a by-election candidate – a potential councillor.

'I'll be out tonight, Lucy,' he repeated, slightly more loudly. 'I've an important party political meeting I *have* to attend. We're going to finalise our manifesto.' Andy said this in a nonchalant, matter-of-fact way, hoping that it would sow a seed of intrigue in Lucy's mind, something she would be unable to resist and which would force her to engage in conversation.

'Wot?'

Andy smiled to himself from behind his paper. This was a promising sign; indeed, the first words from Lucy for three weeks that acknowledged his existence.

'Yes, Lucy. We're finalising our manifesto before the hustings. Need to get leaflets printed: that sort of thing.'

'Wot are you talking about, you fat bastard? Wot's all this about 'ustings and stuff?'

Andy was delighted – she had taken the bait. 'Yeah,' Andy tried to sound casual. '*Oh*! Didn't I tell you? I'm a candidate in the Clapham Common by-election.'

Lucy now entered the room carrying a steaming mug of soup. 'Wot? *You*? Are you standing for the Fat Bastard Party?'

'No, it's a new party, actually.'

'What's it called then?'

Here Andy was in a bit of a quandary. A party called The Beer and Darts Party, although highly appropriate for him and the two other party members, was hardly going to impress a girl who detested Andy's liking for both. 'It's called the BAD Party.' He pronounced the word with a long '*a*' so that it sounded like BARD, the way it's pronounced in the Netherlands.

'What's all that about then. What does it stand for?' Now there was a hint, just a slight hint of interest in Lucy's voice.

Here again, Andy had a credibility gap. The party's manifesto, drawn up during a short break in a darts match and consisting of reducing taxes on beer and fags, might attract the support of fellow boozers, but was hardly likely to impress Lucy. 'Oh – the party's about reducing social injustice, giving more rights to women, making the streets of London safer, ensuring better education for children – that sort of thing,' he said nonchalantly while still peering at his newspaper.

''Ow are you goin' to do that then?' Lucy tried to sound uninterested.

Andy folded his paper and laid it down on the coffee table. He frowned, then, his face creased with *gravitas*, said, 'Well, Lucy, it struck me that there is a great deal of injustice in the world we live in, and rather than just sit around in a pub complaining about it, I decided I should stand up and be counted. Try to do something about it. Even if I get hurt in the process.' Andy glanced discreetly at Lucy and was pleased to see that she was paying attention while pretending not to be interested. 'I've decided to put my head above the parapet, place my neck upon the block, pin my mast to the colours.' Andy was getting his metaphors a little mixed, but his rhetoric was clearly having the desired effect on Lucy.

'I think that's really good, Andy. To be honest, I didn't think you had it in you to do anything useful.'

Andy was now in full flow and enjoying himself. His voice dropped half a tone and, without realising it, he was beginning to sound very slightly like Winston Churchill. 'Lucy,' he said, 'Lucy, it was that girl's murder on the Common that was the final straw. How can I hold my head high in a society where it is not safe to cross a Common? How can I stand proud without attempting to abolish the evil that pervades society? Even if I die in the attempt, it is better to have tried and failed than never to have tried at all. That young girl, not yet cold in her grave, could, I thought, but for chance, have been my housemate, Lucy. It could be *her* lying on that hard slab, not that poor tart Rosie Little.' By now, Andy was getting a little bit carried away, and he suddenly stood up straight, or as straight as he could after sitting on an uncomfortable stool for half an hour, raised the forefinger of his right hand and pointed it at the ceiling. 'Clapham must be a safer, better place. Where is our pride? What has happened to honourable behaviour? Where are the social standards, the moral compasses that should guide us along the stormy path we call life?' Andy, now feeling slightly dizzy from his exertions, sat down once more.

'Ooh! That's lovely, Andy. I think you're really brave saying all that stuff. That made me shiver, that bit about me being on that cold slab, I can tell you. It's a good thing we've got people like you, Andy. Do you really think you can win?'

Andy began to think that he might have overcooked the rhetoric a trifle, but there could be no turning back now. 'Absolutely,' he said. 'It's neck and neck.'

'Tell me, Andy, you didn't shoot that man in the bum deliberately, did you? You know, so that he couldn't sit on the council no more.'

'No, it was a pure but fortuitous accident. It did us both a favour, Lucy. It gave Ponsonby-Titchmarsh an honourable excuse to stand down and me an opportunity to fulfil my destiny.' Once again, Andy pointed at the ceiling.

'Well, Andy, I'm surprised at you.'

Andy smiled to himself and said under his breath, '*Yes*,' but it was just loud enough for Lucy to hear.

'What did you say?'

'Just a tickle in my throat, Lucy.' Andy coughed to prove the point.

'Well, I'm impressed, but you're still a fat bastard.'

'Yes, Lucy, I may be a fat bastard, but at least now I'm a fat bastard with a purpose in life, a fat bastard with a mission, someone who wants to wrong rights.' Andy paused, confused. 'No, that should be to right wrongs.' Then, pleased with his progress and anxious not to lose the high moral ground on which he unexpectedly found himself, he added, 'Anyway, I'm off to the meeting with my team. An evening in politics is a long time, and I need to make the most of it.' He then jumped up once more from his stool, pulled on his tatty old tweed sports jacket and headed purposefully for the door.

'Where's your meeting, Andy?'

'A public meeting place, Lucy. As a registered candidate, I'm allowed to use certain rooms free, as long as I pay for the lighting and heating.' Andy didn't think it necessary to state that the public meeting place he had in mind was the lounge bar of the Nell Gwyn.

'Ooh! That's good. Can I come along?'

Under normal circumstances, Andy would have immediately grasped an opportunity to take Lucy out, but he was concerned that after his political rhetoric and hyperbole, she might be a trifle disappointed when she found a BAD Party meeting consisted of just three people drinking beer in a pub. 'Sorry, Lucy,' he said, 'I would love you to come along, but it's all rather confidential. If our plans get out, it would be dynamite to the other parties and could wreck our chances of success.' Andy was now concerned that he had implied that Lucy was untrustworthy and could not keep a secret. 'I know *you* wouldn't say a word to anyone, but I have the rest of the team to think about. The Party is bigger than the individuals in it – even the candidate himself. That's the way it has to be, Lucy.' By giving the impression that there were several hundred supporters who were relying on him to bring home the metaphorical bacon, Andy desperately hoped that he had retained the ground he had made with Lucy. He needn't have worried.

'Oh, I understand, Andy. I hope your meeting goes well.' Lucy then approached him and brushed a speck of cigarette ash from his sleeve. Andy flushed with delight – for him such a gesture was tantamount to a night of passion. No, he thought to himself, two nights of passion, at least, and it was with a light step that Andy Norris crossed the Common and headed for the Nellie.

***

After Crusher Ericsson had left the guesthouse, the atmosphere suddenly relaxed. Crocker looked at Ivy, ordered a treble whisky, poured it straight down his throat, then requested another. By now, all the tradesmen had left, and as he put his glass down on the bar he heard a gentle ripple of applause from behind him. He turned to see his three fellow residents clapping.

'Well done, Fleur,' said the nurse. 'You were brilliant.'

'Certainly saved us,' added the chambermaid.

'How do you mean?' asked Crocker.

It was the French girl who answered. 'Well, let's just say that Crusher can be a bit unpredictable, and we're all slightly frightened of him.'

'Why? He's big I know, but he may be a gentle giant.'

'That's the problem,' continued the nurse. 'Sometimes he can be really sweet and generous, but then,' and she clicked her fingers to illustrate the suddenness of the change, 'he can be violent and bad-tempered.'

'A Jekyll and Hyde character,' added Ivy from behind the bar, where she was pouring drinks for the residents.

'He seemed to take a shine to you, Fleur. You'll need to be careful.'

'How do you mean?'

'Well' – the chambermaid dropped her voice to a whisper – 'he took a shine to Rosie Little, and look what happened to her.'

'What d'you mean? You think that he...,' Crocker hesitated, not wanting to cause the histrionics he had aroused before, 'did it?'

'He was the last person to see Rosie alive. He said he'd take her out for a drink and that was the last we saw or heard from her.'

Crocker looked at the girls in turn. 'But why don't you tell the police?'

'Fleur,' said the nurse, 'you don't cross Crusher, believe me.'

'We're scared, Fleur,' said the nurse, dabbing the tears from her eyes. 'I don't mind telling you, we're all scared.'

'What's his trade?' asked Crocker, ever the detective.

'What d'you mean?' asked the French girl, who seemed to have lost her Parisian accent once more.'

'Why does he come here? Is he a plumber?'

The residents looked at Fleur with expressions of disbelief on their faces. Ivy responded quickly, 'He does...,' she hesitated, 'a bit of this and that. Fixes things.'

Crocker was thoughtful. 'Ah, I see, an odd job man. Useful person to have about. So you think *he* killed Rosie?'

'Possibly,' said the nurse.

Ivy looked at Crocker knowingly.

'I thought I recognised the man he was talking to. Do you know him?' asked Crocker.

'No idea,' replied the residents in turn.

'Well, I think that's enough excitement for one night,' said Crocker. 'Good night, ladies,' and he headed off to his room.

THIRTEEN

The following Monday, PC Crocker was due to make his first report to the Chief Superintendent. He had decided to leave the guesthouse early, before any of the other residents had woken, so that he wouldn't need to dress as his *alter ego*, Fleur, whose clothes and other accoutrements he packed into a plastic bag to take with him. Once he had left the guesthouse, Crocker found it liberating to be himself again, and he returned to his flat in high spirits, where he was greeted enthusiastically by his cat. There, he washed the remnants of any make-up from his face, donned his uniform and headed for Clapham Police Station.

On entering the familiar reception area, the sergeant on duty looked up and greeted him cordially. 'Crocker, where've you been? I was beginning to think you'd left us for another force.'

'Not allowed to say – classified – you know.' Crocker tapped the side of his nose. 'Is the Chief in?' he asked.

'Yes, is he expecting you?'

'I think so. Could you tell him I'm here?'

'Certainly. Have a seat.'

Crocker sat down and picked up a copy of the previous night's *Evening News*. As he idly thumbed through it, he noticed the picture of a man he vaguely recognised. He began to read.

'Justin Parker, Conservative candidate in the Clapham Common by-election, promises that, if elected, he will make safety a priority. Following the killing of Rosie Little, Mr Parker, pictured above, has promised more police on the beat to ensure that violence of this sort will never happen again. Meanwhile, a police spokesman said that they were following up a number of leads and they hope to make an arrest soon.'

'That's good,' thought Crocker. 'There must have been some progress while I've been undercover.' He studied the picture and was trying to place where he had seen the man, when the desk sergeant informed him that the Chief Super would see him. Crocker stood up, replaced the newspaper and walked smartly into the Chief's office. His senior, dressed impeccably in his neatly-ironed uniform, was sitting in his swivel chair peering at the picture of his passing-out parade which hung on the wall of his office beside him. On hearing Crocker enter, he swivelled round just a trifle too vigorously and on this occasion ended up facing the wall behind his desk.

'Where are you?' he asked, then, realising what had happened, he swivelled back to face Crocker. 'Ah!

There you are. Good to see you back in uniform, Crocker. Take a seat.'

'Thank you, sir.' Crocker marched smartly forward and sat in the chair indicated by the Chief, who continued to peer at him intently.

'Now, Crocker, tell me what's going on. Have you got the murderer yet?'

'Not exactly, sir, but it looks as though you might get him first?'

'What d'you mean, man?'

Crocker was bemused. 'Well, sir, the newspaper stated that the police were following up a number of leads and hope to make an arrest soon.'

'Nonsense, man. We've no leads whatsoever. I told the press that in the knowledge that you were on the case and would be making an arrest soon. *You* are our lead, Crocker, indeed our only hope. Have you been eating enough vegetables?'

'Yes, sir.'

'That's the problem with undercover work; affects your diet, and you know what that can lead to, don't you, Crocker?'

'Yes, sir.'

'And what does it lead to?'

'Irregularity, sir.'

'That's right, Crocker, and you'll never catch a murderer if you're not regular – now will you, Crocker?'

'No, sir.'

'Good. Now tell me what you've managed to find out while you've been undercover in the – ah – guesthouse?'

'Well, sir, not a lot, to be honest, but the residents there—'

Here the Chief frowned, then interrupted. 'The residents?'

'Yes, the other residents. You remember, sir? It's an all-female guesthouse.'

The Chief coughed. 'Ah, yes, of course. I remember now. Had a lot on my mind recently. Now carry on, Crocker.'

'Well, the other residents think that one of the visiting tradesmen, a plumber and odd-job man, I believe, might be the culprit, but I have no concrete evidence yet, sir.'

'That's a shame. What's his name?'

'He goes by the name of Crusher Ericsson, sir. Although I'm beginning to suspect that *Crusher* may not be his real name.'

'Indeed. And what makes you think it might be him?'

'He was the last person Rosie was seen with before her murder.'

'Good, Crocker, that's good. You must befriend this man Crusher and wheedle an admission out of him. Wheedle, that's what we need. Wheedle it out of him.'

'I'll try my best, sir, but I'm concerned that he's a violent man.'

'And you're a highly trained police officer, Crocker. You can wheedle.'

'But I think he might have taken a shine to me, sir.'

'How d'you mean, a shine?'

'Well, he said I was different to the other girls.'

'Girls, Crocker, what are you on about? Are you sure you're regular – peristaltically speaking?'

'Yes, sir. It's not me he's taken a shine to, it's Fleur.'

The Chief's expression suddenly relaxed. 'Of course, Crocker. Don't sound so surprised. You're a very attractive woman – well, man.' The Chief Super frowned with confusion. 'You know what I mean.'

'Thank you, sir.'

'The situation is perfect for a bit of wheedling. Urge him on, Crocker. Flirt and wheedle. Flirt and wheedle, in that order. Got it, Crocker?'

'Yes, sir.'

'What are you going to do?'

'Flirt and wheedle, sir.'

'Spot on. Can you do that?'

'I'll try, sir.'

'I need a result. There's a lot of pressure on me to get an arrest because of this damned by-election.'

'Of course, sir.'

'By the way, Crocker, that man you worked with a couple of years ago on the case of the shot tramp is running for some type of loony party.'

'What? Andy Norris?' said Crocker, surprised.

'Yes, that's the man.'

'Oh!' Crocker's eyes suddenly widened and his gaze focused somewhere on the wall behind the Chief Super's head. He had just realised why he recognised the man whose picture he had seen in the *Evening News*. He cried out involuntarily. '*Aaah.*'

The Chief Super was taken aback and immediately sat bolt upright in his chair. 'What on earth's the matter, man?'

'I know where I saw him now.'

'You're talking in riddles, man. Saw who? Norris?'

'No. The candidate.'

'What are you talking about, Crocker?'

'The other candidate. Let me get the paper.'

'Are you mad?'

'No, it's important to the case.'

Crocker stood up, dashed to the door and into reception, where he grabbed the copy of the *Evening News* he had been reading earlier, from an old man who had been attempting the crossword. With a cursory, 'Sorry, essential evidence,' shouted in the general direction of the old man, he rushed back into the Chief's office, opened the newspaper at the appropriate page and indicated the article he had been reading earlier. 'It's him, sir.'

'What's him, Crocker? Talk sense, man.'

Crocker pointed to the picture of Justin Parker. 'It's him. That's the man who was talking to Crusher in the guesthouse. Crusher said he had some business to do for him, something about canvassing.'

On hearing this, the Chief's eyes widened and momentarily he allowed his imagination to wander. Chief Constable, Sir Cecil Winterbottom, he thought to himself. 'Say that again, Crocker.'

***

The following day, the headlines in the *Evening News* revealed that the Tory candidate in the forthcoming by-election had links with the underworld and was suspected of associating with violent criminals with the intention of influencing the outcome of the election. The very next day, Crocker read with interest how Justin Parker, the Conservative candidate in the Clapham Common by-election, had withdrawn from the electoral contest. While declaring his complete innocence of all the accusations made against him, he said he felt he could not remain a candidate while an investigation was pending. The article concluded that with the withdrawal of the Conservative candidate, the race was now between the Liberal and Labour parties. Andy Norris, who had also read the article was relieved that his party, the BAD Party, and the Martian Party were only briefly mentioned as the other parties fielding a candidate.

Crocker was puzzled. 'That's strange,' he thought. 'What a coincidence. That's just what I was discussing with the Chief yesterday. The press have been very astute to pick up on this so quickly.'

Having been away from his undercover mission for three days, Crocker realised he had to get back to the guesthouse, so on Thursday he donned his skirt, blouse and wig, applied his make-up liberally and returned there.

***

'Grand job, Cecil, or should I say...' – Bill Bishop smiled at the Chief Superintendent slyly – '*Sir* Cecil?' They were seated in the Chief Super's office and the Labour candidate was beaming from ear to ear.

'Thank you, ah, Bill. Yes, it did work out rather well as it happens.'

'I don't want to know how you stitched 'im up. Better that way, but you certainly did a good job. I wonder 'ow the newspapers got hold of it.'

'Mm. Yes, it was quite uncanny how they were on to him as quick as a flash. Astute journalism, I'd say.' The Chief was thoughtful for a moment. 'I just wish they'd be less critical of me and my chaps over the Rosie Little murder.'

'Yes, Cecil, it would be good if that were to be solved; but, to be honest,' and here the Labour candidate looked the policeman in the eye, 'politically it would be better if it were solved after the election, that is, if I win.'

'Ah, why is that?'

'That way I can criticise you and your chaps during the campaign, saying you're all lazy bastards and not up to the job: rant on about cutbacks and all that sort of guff – demand better policing...' On seeing the surprise on the Chief's face, Bill Bishop added, 'Nothing personal, mind; then afterwards, once elected, hey presto, we find our killer and I can take the credit. That's assuming I'm the winner, which, by the way, is now quite likely as you eliminated the only other serious candidate, leaving that wishy-washy, pinko Liberal, who hardly counts. So I thought I'd just pop in and congratulate you on a job well done.'

'Thank you, Bill. Ah yes, it did work out rather well, although, of course, I had nothing whatsoever to do with it, you understand.'

'Of course not. Mum's the word.' Bill Bishop tapped the side of his nose. 'Well, I can see you're a busy man, so I'll be off. Campaigns to run, colleagues to rubbish, that sort of thing. I'll be seeing you, *Chief* Constable, after the election.' The Labour candidate then rose to his feet and walked smartly to the door of the office, slamming it shut behind him, leaving the Chief smiling contentedly to himself as he once more perused the passing-out parade of 1956.

FOURTEEN

''Ow did your meetin' go?' Lucy, who was making a sandwich in the kitchen, shouted through the serving hatch to Andy, who was in the lounge, perched on his bar stool while reading a newspaper. It was the day the story of the Conservative candidate's resignation had broken. Andy had not seen Lucy since the night of his Party meeting, as she had been staying with her friend Lucinda at her apartment in Chelsea.

'Very well, actually. We finalised our manifesto, printed some leaflets and have started canvassing.'

''Ave you worked out how to make the streets of Clapham safer then?'

'Well, the first thing is to get elected, and then we can work on the details.' Andy was becoming more than a trifle worried that his eloquence might backfire. He knew that as long as there wasn't a hope in hell of him being elected, he wouldn't need to respond to idiotic questions like this and could simply rely on his previously unrecognised talent for sophistry to impress Lucy. If, for some reason, she discovered that his policies were non-existent and dreamt-up during the break in a darts match, then his plan to woo her would reach an early and sudden demise. He needed to appear wholly sincere in his ambitions in the run-up to the election and then seem totally bereft when he lost, in the knowledge that he had been denied the opportunity to fulfil his goal of making the world – well, Clapham Common at any rate – a better place.

'You'll be pleased to hear about the Tory toff then?'

'What about him?' asked Andy, surprised that Lucy knew anything about the candidates.

'You must 'ave 'eard. He's withdrawn from the race because he's being investigated for something or other. Lucinda told me about it. I even read the article, and your party was mentioned. I was evva so proud. I said to Lucinda, "That's Andy and the BAD Party: 'e's their candidate." And she said in 'er high-falutin' voice, "But Andrew doesn't know anything about politics," an' I said, "I know, but he's got some great ideas about safe streets and stuff." Then she said, "Well, maybe knowing nothing about politics is the best starting point for an aspiring councillor. A completely vacuous mind, allied to the ability to shoot other councillors in the backside, might just be exactly the right qualifications for a successful career in politics. It's certainly more gentlemanly than *knifing* one's colleagues in the back." Any'ow, she was going to support the toff, but now 'e's out of the race, I've got them thinking that it might be best if she and Rupert came out in favour of you. That would be good, wouldn't it?'

Andy, sitting on his bar stool, was uneasy about this development, but dared not show it. He really wanted as few people as possible to know about his political ambitions, or rather lack of them. The more people that knew, the likelier it was that it would be discovered that he and his party were a fraud – the whole thing a cynical scam, set up with the sole aim of getting Lucy to go to bed with him.

'Yes, that would be tremendous,' Andy lied, 'but I mustn't take advantage of the fact that they're friends of yours.'

'Not at all. They think it's great that finally you're doing something useful with your life. Lucinda said she'd be happy to 'elp with speech-writing or rallies, stuff like that. Rupert can't officially help as 'e's in the 'Ouse of Lords, but secretly he'll support you. "Anything to keep Labour and the Liberals out," he said.'

'He might want to support the Martian Party?' suggested Andy hopefully.

'Wot? That loony? You must be joking. No, there's only one alternative party with any credibility, Andy, and that's yours.'

Andy's heart sank as he heard this. Then he thought to himself, there's not a hope in hell of winning, so all I've got to do is keep my head low for three weeks until I lose the election and it'll all be over. 'Thanks, Lucy,' he said, 'that's really helpful. You've been great, but you mustn't get your hopes too high as it's just possible that I may not win.'

'You've got to think positive, Andy. You can do it if you try. Think positive.' Lucy entered the lounge, where she took a seat and began to eat.

'Yes, you're right, Lucy. I have to believe. I have to believe it's possible. I must be confident that I can fulfil my destiny – to heal this fractured society, without thought or consideration for myself.' Andy's lower lip protruded and his voice dropped a tone as he wagged his finger at the ceiling light, causing him to wobble precariously on his stool. 'I must fight and fight as no one has fought before.'

'Ooh! That's lovely, Andy.'

***

PC Crocker, or Fleur as he now was, having resumed his disguise, had been welcomed back to the guesthouse by the other residents as an old friend. She had been hugged by all the girls and was now standing at the bar with the nurse, the chambermaid and the French girl, having a drink. On his enquiring, the girls had confirmed that Crusher had been in on several occasions during the week, but had stayed only long enough to ascertain whether or not he, or rather she, Fleur, was in residence, before leaving, sometimes without even having a drink.

It was eight o'clock and it had been a quiet evening thus far, with only one tradesman popping in to do a job. Suddenly, the door banged open and in walked Crusher. The other residents instantly became tense and nervous; and even Ivy, who was standing behind the bar, appeared to move a pace backwards. Crocker similarly was alert. He remembered the Chief's words, 'Flirt and wheedle, flirt and wheedle, in that order.' Or was it wheedle and flirt? He didn't really understand what his boss had meant, but he remembered clearly the nurse saying that the last person to see Rosie alive had been Crusher, who had taken a shine to her, as he now had to him.

Crocker looked at the big man who had just entered the bar. There was something different about him. Crocker looked at him, trying to ascertain what it was that had changed. Then it struck him – he looked well-dressed. No longer the unkempt hair and three-day stubble, Crusher was now clean-shaven and his wild hair was neatly slicked down. Instead of a dirty T-shirt and jeans, he was wearing a suit and a shirt and tie. As he came closer, Crocker noticed two other things: firstly, he smelled strongly of Brut aftershave, and secondly, he was carrying a large bunch of flowers. Crusher approached almost hesitantly and when still about a yard from Crocker halted and held out the flowers. 'Fleur,' he said nervously, 'these are for you.'

Crocker faltered, not sure what the best course of action might be. 'Flirt and wheedle.' *What on earth did the Chief mean by that?* he wondered. Almost by reflex, he reached out and took the flowers. 'Thanks, Crusher,' he said, admiring the bouquet, 'they're lovely.'

Crusher's face creased with pleasure. 'They're chrysanthemums, Fleur.' Crusher fell silent for a moment, unsure what to say next. 'The lady in the flower shop said you should put them in water as soon as possible.' He hesitated again, nervously wringing his hands. 'It's good to see you, Fleur. I thought you might have disappeared out of my life. Where 'ave you been?'

'Business, Crusher, business. You know how it is.'

Crusher smiled. 'I like that, Fleur. Not just a pretty face. I bet you've had your fingers in a few pies.'

'You could say that.'

'Entrepreneur, that's what you are, I reckon. I like that in a girl. Now, what'll you have to drink?'

'A pint, please.'

'That's my girl.' Crusher looked to the proprietress behind the bar. 'Make that two, Ivy.'

Seeing his opportunity, Crocker said nonchalantly, 'And how's your business going, Crusher? You had a job on last time I saw you.'

'Fell through, Fleur. Can't tell you details, but my sponsor pulled out.'

'I'm sorry, but that's business, isn't it, Crusher?'

'That's right. You've just got to pick yourself up, dust yourself off...'

Crocker interrupted and began to sing, 'And start all over again.'

Crusher chuckled, a sound like gravel in a rotating cement mixer. 'Yeah, that's it.' He then paused for a moment as if uncertain and nervous. 'Fleur, I've been meaning to say, my name's not really Crusher.'

'*No*?'

'I know "Crusher" suits me, but my real name is...' The big man paused again, unsure of himself, before adding quietly, 'Jeremy.' He then looked at Fleur and in a more confident voice said, 'Jeremy... Small. Don't tell anyone, will you? In my line of work, Jeremy Small isn't an ideal *nom de plume*, as it were, and Crusher Ericsson is better for business. Gets more respect, know wot I mean? But I'd like *you* to call me Jeremy.'

'That's fine, er, Jeremy,' Crocker replied.

A tear came into Crusher's eye. 'No one has called me that since me mum passed away. Fell down the stairs – pissed as a newt, she was. Brings it all back.' Crocker stood quietly, not knowing what to say. 'Anyway, Fleur, I'd like to take you out, maybe go for a meal. There's a nice little café across the Common. Would you come out with me?'

The mention of the Common made Crocker flinch. He was frightened that Dr Jekyll, or rather Jeremy Small, might turn into Mr Hyde, or rather Crusher Ericsson in the middle of the Common, and he might end up on the same cold slab as Rosie. Then there was the problem of what would happen when Jeremy, Crusher, or whatever he called himself – who certainly had his fair share of testosterone, his bulging muscles were testament to that – tried to seduce him. Crocker had led a sheltered life and was sexually inexperienced, but he knew that it would come as a nasty shock when Crusher discovered that he, the person Crusher thought of as Fleur, was, in fact, a man in woman's clothing. A surprise like that was likely to unhinge the most equable of men, let alone one known to have a volatile temper. Yet Crocker still had to find out if this man was the murderer. He began to feel sick. Crocker then recalled the inevitable response he had received on numerous occasions when he had asked girls out. He poured down the remains of his beer and faced Jeremy.

'Crusher,' he began, 'I mean Jeremy, you're a dear, dear man. I love the flowers, chrysanthemums are my favourite, but this has been so sudden. I'm a girl who needs time to make such an important decision – someone who gives a lot of thought before going out with a man. I don't want you to think I'm a pushover, a girl who'll do anything for a free meal. I don't want you to think of me as someone without any standards or morals. I'll need time to think about your kind offer.'

To begin with, Crusher was puzzled, confused by the unexpected refusal, and then his surprise began to turn to annoyance. Crocker sensed the anger building up in the giant man and was waiting for that massive spade of a fist to bury itself in the side of his head. Then an amazing thing happened. Crusher's face dissolved into a wide smile and he took Crocker's hands in his own. 'Fleur,' he said, 'I respect that. I respect that in a girl.

Someone with high moral standards is unusual, particularly in a place like this. I like that in a girl.'

Crocker could hardly believe his luck and began to breathe more easily. 'I'm glad you understand, Jeremy. I mustn't be rushed.'

'I understand, Fleur. I promise I won't rush you. But I hope you'll allow me to come and visit you again?'

'Of course, Jeremy, of course,' replied Crocker, hoping that the relief he felt inside was not reflected in his voice.

Crusher bowed his head and Crocker could feel a tear drop onto his hand. 'I've never met anyone like you,' he said.

'I bet you haven't,' said Crocker with feeling, before adding belatedly, 'nor me you.'

'Right, dearest, I'm going, before I get carried away. I have to leave town for a week or so – business, you know – but I'll be back next week to see you.' With that, Crusher dropped Crocker's hands, turned and walked purposefully out of the bar and once again into the Clapham night.

As Crusher left, a couple of workmen entered the bar and started speaking to the nurse and the French girl.

Crocker chatted to Ivy for a while and then decided to go to bed. As he passed down the hallway, he heard some muffled noises from a closed doorway on his left. He was about to ascend the stairs to his bedroom when the noises grew louder and he recognised the squeals of distress and pain. Crocker decided that it was his responsibility as a policeman to investigate.

FIFTEEN

'The problem is, Zeph, that I think I might have overdone it a bit. You know, over-egged my political aspirations just a tad. Raised expectations too high.'

'How d'you mean, man?'

'Well, Lucy now thinks I'm the best thing since Winston Churchill and that I'm going to change the world.'

'Why does she think that, man?'

'Probably because I told her so.'

'But she knows you're just a fat, lazy bastard.'

'Yes, but now she thinks I'm a fat, lazy bastard with a mission.'

Zephaniah turned his gaze from the newspaper he was reading to look at Andy. 'That's okay, that's what you wanted. You wanted to impress her, and that's what you gone an' done.'

The Herald Lounge Bar was busy with Friday after-work drinkers and the jukebox was blaring out 'Bohemian Rhapsody'.

'Yes, but the problem is what happens when she finds out that the BAD Party consists of you and me?'

'That's not true. There's the other member, what's 'is name?'

'Well, there is Ted, but that still hardly constitutes a political force to be reckoned with, and Lucy seems to think that we actually have a chance of winning.'

'*What?* I thought she was sensible. Why does she think that?'

Andy took a swig of lager. 'Well, it's just possible that I might have given her that impression – accidentally.'

'You is right up the creek, man. But there ain't no need to worry, as there's no way you'll get any votes. Now that the Tory toff has withdrawn, it's between that Labour man and the weedy Liberal.' Zephaniah was thoughtful for a moment. 'Tell me, man, why is it that Liberals are all weedy and Labour candidates all fat bastards like you?'

'That's just a political stereotype, Zeph.'

'What's that?'

'Unfounded perceptions.'

'If that's the case, then is that Martian candidate all green with funny ears?'

'No one has ever seen him. I'm not even sure he exists.'

'He's a real loony then?'

'Appears so, Zeph.' Andy sipped disconsolately at his pint. 'Anyway, what are we going to do?'

'You don' need to do nothin', man. Just turn up, lose the election and then pretend you're disappointed.'

'I suppose so, but I *am* getting a bit worried. Lucy and her posh friends keep asking me about policies and things. I can hardly tell them we don't have any.'

'But we do, man. You said so. You told me you got a manifesto and everythin'.'

'True, but cutting the tax on beer and fags is hardly going to cut much ice with Lucy and her pals. Then there are the hustings coming up. I'm going to have to think of something to say!'

'Don' matter what you say, man. No one ever listens. Politicians don' make no sense to ordinary people, and even if they did, it don' matter, as they do something different once they is elected, man. Don' worry, just relax an' get me a drink, man, it's nearly time for me to go to work.'

After returning from the bar with fresh drinks, Andy continued, 'Maybe we should do a bit of canvassing?'

'What's that?' Zephaniah picked up his rum and Coke and took a sip.

'Well, as far as I can gather, it's knocking on doors, distributing leaflets and asking people to vote for you.'

'That's easy. I could do that, man. Tell you what, I'll put some of them leaflets through doors on my way to work.'

Andy thought for a moment. 'No, Zeph, that's no good, they've got to live in the Clapham Common constituency to be able to vote in the by-election.'

'I ain't goin' there, man. Anyway, I thought you didn't want any votes?'

Andy picked up his pint and managed to pour half of the contents down the front of his suit. 'Look at that,' he exclaimed, looking down at the beer stain. 'I'm a nervous wreck. I'm beginning to wish I hadn't got involved with all this malarkey.'

'But remember, man, you said you wanted to run the country. You said you could do better than the Muppets what are doin' it now.'

Andy just shook his head, unsure as to how he'd managed to get himself into this mess, and even less certain how he would get himself out of it.

Back at Parkview, later on that evening, Andy was greeted by Lucy. 'You're late, Andy. Been canvassing?'

Andy, smelling strongly of beer and holding the remains of his large portion of fish and chips in his hand, went into the lounge and looked longingly at where the settee used to be. He then wearily took his position on the bar stool, where he promptly spilt the remains of his supper into his lap. 'Yeah, busy night,' he shouted in the general direction of the kitchen, where Lucy was washing-up.

'I've got some really good news, Andy – you'll never guess what,' replied Lucy.

Andy was immediately alert. Good news from Lucy usually meant trouble for him. Andy was even beginning to think that life was easier when Lucy hated him with a passion and refused to talk to him. 'Oh yes?' he said.

'Yeah, Lucinda wants to be your campaign manager. She's got all sorts of friends in high places. None of them lives round 'ere, of course, but she's decided to knock on some doors in the safer parts of the neighbourhood and canvass on your behalf. That's good, innit?'

'That's really great,' said Andy with an enthusiasm he far from felt.

'She was wondering if she could have some of your leaflets?'

Andy groaned. He did have some leaflets. But they were cheap photocopies stating that the Beer and Darts Party was a one-agenda-item party with the sole aim of reducing tax on beer and cigarettes. 'I'm afraid we've run out, Lucy, and the party funds have dried up completely. That's a real shame.'

'I'm sure she could arrange for some more to be printed.' Lucy then entered the room carrying a mug of coffee and sat down. 'Isn't it exciting, Andy. You about to be a councillor an' all. You seem awfully calm. Aren't you just a little bit excited?'

'Not really,' answered Andy honestly.

'Then there's that debate next week. What d'you call it?'

'The hustings.'

'Yeah. You must be really nervous. 'Ave you decided what you're going to say?'

In reality, Andy was in a state of utter terror at the very idea of delivering his non-existent policies to a room full of people, including the press. 'More or less,' Andy lied. 'Just a few final bits and pieces to rehearse.'

'Well, Andy, tomorrow's Saturday and I've cancelled all my arrangements so Lucinda and I can help you out. Just let us know what you want us to do.'

Andy groaned quietly to himself and for a fleeting moment thought of owning up, before saying, 'That's great, Lucy, really helpful. We'll decide tomorrow what our best plan of attack is. I need to go to party headquarters first thing and we can discuss tactics when I return.'

'You see, Ted, it's all gone tits up. Everyone seems to expect me to win this bloody by-election and for me to actually achieve something. Life was much easier when no one expected anything of me and I was just a fat, lazy bastard.'

'But you are a fat, lazy bastard. Nothing's changed there, Andy.'

It was the following morning and Andy was in the BAD Party headquarters – the public bar of the Nell Gwyn – having his first pint of the day with the party chairman.

'I can't tell them that the BAD Party stands for beer and darts and that we've no policies whatsoever.'

Ted was drying glasses and placing them neatly on shelves behind him. 'There's the tax reduction programme.'

'Yes, but reducing taxes on beer and fags hardly constitutes a policy that will impress Lucy and her pals.'

'We could reinvent ourselves.' Ted started to set up the bar ready for the Saturday lunchtime trade.

'What d'you mean, reinvent ourselves?'

'Well, how many people know what BAD *actually* stands for?'

'No one apart from us.'

'That's you, me and Zephaniah, right?'

'Yes.' Andy looked at Ted, puzzled.

'Well, let's rename it.' Ted thought for a while. 'How about the Bad And Good Party?'

'No, that spells BAG, and everyone knows it's BAD, pronounced BARD.'

'Oh yeah.' Ted stood still, thoughtful for a while, before his face creased into a smile. 'I know. How about Birth And Death Party.'

Andy was thoughtful for a moment. 'That does have a ring to it,' he admitted.

'It sounds like a proper party, you know – serious. And it would be great for slogans like,' Ted hesitated for a moment, '"Be safe from birth to death with the BAD Party", or "We'll look after you from Birth to Death". There's loads of possibilities.'

Andy finished his beer. 'Ted, you're brilliant. You have a real gift for this sort of thing. I'll need to get some more leaflets printed.'

'Perhaps you'd better rewrite them as well.'

'Yeah, good idea. "Smoke and drink? Vote for the BAD Party" hardly seems appropriate any more: sends out the wrong message to the likes of Lucy and Lucinda. Thanks, Ted, I'll pop into work and get some printed off straight away.'

SIXTEEN

Crocker could not control his curiosity. He slowly tiptoed back down the corridor and listened outside the closed door from where the strange sounds had emanated. He placed his ear against the door and heard a bizarre rhythmic squeaking sound, as though something was gently swinging, accompanied by an occasional muffled sobbing sound. He decided to peek through the keyhole. Crocker could see little of the dim interior, yet did detect that something inside seemed to be swinging – casting an oscillating shadow on the far wall of the room. Then he heard a voice he recognised. ''Ave you had enough yet?' The thick French accent of the Parisian girl was unmistakable. Crocker stood up from the listening position he had assumed and smiled to himself. He needn't have worried: this was just another of the odd-job men earning a bit of overtime, probably replacing a light bulb, he thought to himself as he began once more to head for the stairs and his room.

'You 'ave been vair naughty man – you deserve more. You need to be punished.' There followed a swishing sound and then a muffled shout. 'Zere, 'ave you 'ad enough *now*?'

Crocker, now motionless in the hallway, could not hear the answer. Then there came a further swishing sound, followed by a whimper. 'You deserve zat. Now I'm getting vairy angry. I leave you to 'tink what I do next.' He then heard steps heading towards the door and Crocker quickly ducked under the staircase where he would not be seen by anyone leaving the room. Sure enough, the door opened and the French girl came out and headed for the bar, lighting a cigarette as she did so.

'That's strange,' thought Crocker to himself, 'I wonder what's going on in there?'

Crocker hesitated. He didn't know what to do. He had no reason to suspect the French girl of any misdemeanours, but her behaviour and what he had heard of the conversation had been strange. What could she mean by, 'You deserve more'? Could this be a lead? Could whoever the French girl was talking to be the murderer of Rosie Little? Maybe they had the suspect tied up and were trying to beat a confession out of him. This might just be the opportunity for him to crack this case wide open. Crocker smiled to himself. 'Got you,' he whispered to himself as he crept out from his hiding place and walked quietly back to the room from where the creaking and squeaking could still be heard. He gingerly turned the handle, opened the door and stepped inside. The room was lit by candles, and initially all he could detect was what appeared to be a large sack swinging from the ceiling.

As his eyes grew accustomed to the dark, he realised that what he thought was a sack was, in fact, a cargo net which was hanging from a pulley attached to a large exposed beam. When he looked more closely, he noticed that the net contained something pink, shaped rather like a large foetus. Then he jumped back in alarm as he realised that the large pink thing was a man: a man tied up, completely naked and swinging gently. Crocker could see livid weals on his plump buttocks. Crocker was motionless, speechless for a moment, then he let out a low scream: 'Aaarh.'

The noise alerted the man in the net to the presence of someone in the room and, after straining to see who it was, on spotting Crocker, he said calmly, 'Who the 'ell are you? Where's Fifi?'

Crocker, initially wrong-footed by his discovery, said to himself quietly, 'Steady, Crocker: remember your training.' He now knew exactly what had been going on in the guesthouse. It was as clear as day. How could he have been so stupid not to see it before? The other residents had known all along who Rosie's murderer was, then had captured him, strung him up and were intent on getting a confession out of him. 'You've got to hand it to the girls,' he thought.

Crocker looked up at the man in the net. 'Right,' he said in his most official voice, 'I'm PC Crocker and you're under arrest. I'm going to get you down, but don't make any attempt to escape,' then inexplicably adding, 'I'm armed.'

To Crocker's surprise, the man showed no alarm, but simply said in a strong Northern accent, 'I don't care 'oo *you* are, I've got another fifteen minutes with Fifi.'

'What d'you mean, you've got another fifteen minutes?'

'Look, darlin', I paid for an hour and by jove, I'm goin' to get my hour. So you just run along and fetch that French tart. I need some more punishment.'

'Ah!'

'Look, just do as you're told and get Fifi. There's a good girl.'

'Ah!'

'Look, I don't know who you are, but tell the French tart that I'm ready for me punishment, will you?'

I think I have said earlier in this tale that Crocker was not the most worldly-wise, nor intellectually the most gifted of men. He had put two and two together and come up with four hundred and sixty. His conclusion, which, not surprisingly, was entirely erroneous, was that the swinging man was the murderer and that he was being detained by a bunch of residents in the guesthouse. The ridiculousness of this theory would be immediately apparent to any unbiased observer with even a modicum of intelligence, but this was PC Crocker, and it was the conclusion that he, alias Fleur, had adopted, and as such, once reached, could not be reconsidered. However, now the swinging man was not behaving in a manner consistent with this theory. When Crocker's brain couldn't comprehend a situation, its response was to shut down completely, rather as a computer does when it becomes overloaded, or when, in an overheated petrol engine, the pistons seize up and weld themselves to the cylinder. His jaw dropped as far as it anatomically could and he stood rigid, frozen to the spot. His cerebral cortex had shut down as a result of the overload of incomprehensible information it had received in the last five minutes and all constructive mental activity had ceased – he was catatonic. It is difficult to find the correct adjective to describe his state of mind in that moment, but the reader might choose some of the following: poleaxed, perplexed; dumbfounded, astounded; stupefied, speechless; bewildered and amazed. If, dear reader, I have given you the impression that PC Crocker had totally lost it, then I have succeeded in my task.

No one knows how long Crocker stood, stock-still, whimpering, while the swinging, naked man urged him to fetch Fifi, but eventually Crocker heard footsteps, the door swung open and the French girl entered.

'Oh, hello, Fleur,' she said. 'I didn't know you were into this sort of thing.'

'Ugh!' was all Crocker could articulate.

'Giving him some extra punishment? Fine by me, dear, but I'd better take over again now.' The French girl looked at Fleur and smiled. 'Just nipped out for a fag.'

'Ah!'

'You can watch if you want.'

'Ugh!'

The girl turned her attention to the swinging man. 'You az been vairy naughty, I vill have to punish you.'

Crocker, dazed as he was, registered that the girl who he now knew was called Fifi, was sounding more German than French. She then picked up a short riding crop and bent it between her hands in full view of the man.

It was then that Crocker found his voice. 'I was going to arrest him.'

Fifi pursed her lips thoughtfully. 'That would be something new,' she said. 'Maybe next time.' The French girl then brought the crop down hard on the man's buttocks. 'Zat will teach you,' she said as the man whimpered quietly.

Crocker headed in a daze towards the door, and after another lashing he heard his fellow-resident say, 'See you later, Fleur,' and he closed the door behind him.

Upstairs in his room, Crocker attempted to unscramble his brains and make some sense of the evening.

Crocker tried, but he couldn't sleep. Strange, disconnected thoughts whirled about his brain. Why on earth would a respectable resident of the guesthouse, albeit French, string a man up, naked, from the ceiling and punish him, if it wasn't for the murder of poor Rosie Little? Why didn't she simply hand him over to the police? He admitted to himself that he could never bring himself to take seriously anyone who belonged to a race that ate snails for pleasure, but whipping a naked man who was hanging from the ceiling in a net was quite incomprehensible, even for someone of Gallic extraction. And why didn't the man accept his offer of salvation? Who was the murderer of Rosie Little, and was Crusher Ericsson the *alter ego* of Jeremy Small? He just couldn't make any sense of it. Eventually, Crocker decided he would pop downstairs for a glass of water.

He walked along the corridor, past the door to the room where he had witnessed the strange events of the evening, and pushed open the door to the bar. In his disturbed state of mind it hadn't occurred to him that there might be anyone else still awake, and he had not taken the trouble to put on his wig. He had just slipped on his dressing gown and his face still bore the remains of his make-up, making him look rather like a slightly camp, balding, middle-aged homosexual. As he entered the bar, he heard voices and saw the backs of two men who were sitting on bar stools, while, facing him, standing behind the bar, Ivy was pouring drinks. She was thus the first of the trio to notice Crocker. She stared at the strange-looking person until after a moment her puzzled expression gave way to one of recognition. 'Oh! Hello, Fleur,' she said. 'D'you want a drink?'

'Thanks, Ivy. I just came down for a glass of water. I couldn't sleep because of all that's been going on. I've been seeing some strange things, Ivy. I'm beginning to think I might be going mad.'

'What *you* need is a drink. Come and join us.'

As PC Crocker walked across the room to the bar, the two men turned to greet him and it was then that Crocker had his second total mental collapse of the evening.

SEVENTEEN

'Lucinda's coming round at four o'clock for a campaign meetin'.' Lucy, who was in the kitchen making lunch, shouted this through the serving hatch.

'Oh, good!' Andy tried to sound enthusiastic. It was Saturday afternoon and he had returned to Parkview with the newly revised leaflets and rejuvenated Party manifesto.

'She wants to discuss strategy and stuff.'

'That's great.' In fact, Andy was now much more sanguine about the future as that morning he had seen a poll which put the Labour candidate twenty points ahead of the Liberal, and neither he nor his opponent in the Martian Party had featured at all. He knew that he could now go through the motions, pretend to be interested in this farce that he had created and then be a noble loser when the time came. Nothing could possibly go wrong, he thought to himself. He then shouted back, 'I'll need to put the finishing touches to my speech later on. It's important for me to get just the right balance of sincerity without appearing to be sanctimonious.'

'Ooh, you can do that, Andy, that's what you're good at – you know sanctimonious 'an all. Want a coffee?'

'Yes, please.'

'Twenty sugars?'

'If that's all there is.'

The doorbell rang just as Lucy was handing Andy his coffee. 'I'll get it,' she said, and a moment later Lucy ushered Lucinda into the lounge.

'Andrew, how good to see you.' Lucinda shook his hand. 'You never cease to amaze me; I'm immensely proud of you. There's no hope of you winning, of course, but we must put up a fight against the Labour chappy. He's not a nice man.'

'Couldn't agree more, Lucinda. We must do everything in our power to rid ourselves of this monster, this evil in our society, this pustule we call socialism.'

Lucinda, quite taken aback by Andy's eloquence, simply said, 'Quite.'

'You see, Lucinda,' Lucy turned to her friend, 'I said 'e was good with words, didn't I?'

'Quite.'

'And another thing, Lucinda, Andy and the BADs *can* win. You're neck and neck, aren't you, Andy?'

'Well, I, ah...' Andy hesitated, not sure whether or not to mention the poll.

'Course you can, you've just got to be positive.'

'Quite.' Lucinda didn't want to dampen Lucy's enthusiasm. 'Quite,' she said again. She was dressed in what she perceived to be an outfit appropriate for canvassing, which consisted of a layer of tweed covered by a long waxed coat and a pair of green wellington boots.

'Now, Andrew, where are those leaflets? We must press on at once if we are to have any chance of closing the gap.' Andy passed a leaflet to her, which Lucinda read with interest. 'So that's what BAD stands for: Birth and Death. That's very good, Andrew. It really sticks in one's mind. What's your policy on the NHS?'

'Keep it.'

'Yes, I think that's wise.'

Andy looked at Lucinda thoughtfully. 'Do you think I should mention the war?'

'Mmm. That's difficult.' Lucinda hesitated. 'Probably not, unless someone else mentions it first. It might be unwise to make it a major campaign issue. Now, how are you going to attack the Labour chappy's policies? He's ahead in the polls and needs to be neutralised.'

'Isn't that a bit harsh?' asked Andy.

'How do you mean?'

'I mean, are you allowed to neutralise your opposition?'

'I meant neutralise his policies; not kill him.' Lucinda tutted. 'You have to ridicule him, make him look stupid – which shouldn't be difficult. He *is* from Yorkshire after all.'

'Mmm.' Andy was in uncharted territory and didn't know what to say. He was desperately trying to impress Lucy, but in reality hadn't a clue what Lucinda was talking about. He said, 'Mmm,' once more while looking at the floor, his hand over his mouth, trying to look thoughtful and intelligent while his mind was a complete blank. Suddenly, his eyes lit up with a hint of intelligence and he said, almost excitedly, 'I know! We could ask what a Yorkshireman is doing in Clapham. You know, something like: "Keep Clapham for Londoners. Northerners go home".'

'I do wish you would call it Clarm, Andrew, Clapham is *so* common.'

'I know, Lucinda,' interrupted Lucy, ''ow about, "Keep Clapham Common". Geddit?'

'Lucinda, if I called it Clarm, no one apart from you and Rupert would know what on earth I was talking about,' said Andy.

'Oh well, Clapham it must be then. But, Andrew, I like the "Northerner go home" message. There are far too many of them down here already; I saw one only yesterday: in *Chelsea*, for heaven's sake. What *are* things coming to? That's why we need someone like you on the council, Andrew. Someone with a complete absence of ideas, no real policies at all, someone who won't do any damage to the establishment.'

'*That's it*, Lucinda. Everyone else bangs on about improving things. With me on the council, however, the great Clapham electorate will know nothing whatsoever will change, that I am completely deficient in the old ideas department. Our slogan could be, "Vote for the *status quo*, vote BAD".'

'Andrew, that's rather good.'

'But, Andy, wot about making the world, or at least Clapham, a safer place? That's wot you said you'd do.' Lucy looked disappointed.

'Lucy, you're right, I mustn't forget my mission, my ideals, my...,' Andy looked skywards, 'my goals to help humanity, children and doddery old ladies in particular.'

'That's lovely, Andy. Isn't it, Lucinda?'

'Quite.'

'Then there's our tax reduction policy. That should get the popular vote.'

'Yes, reducing tax on champagne and cigars is undoubtedly a vote-winning policy. I think you've done very well, Andrew. Now, I suggest we knock on a few doors and meet up later in the pub for a drink. I'll take the north side of the Common, where it's a bit posher. You two can handle the south and west.'

That is how the unlikely trio of Lucinda (or Lady Forsyth as she was now known), Lucy and Andy went leaflet-posting late on a Saturday afternoon. And, of course, it was inevitable that it would be Lucinda who walked up the drive to an all-female guesthouse to canvass opinions on the forthcoming by-election and that the person who answered the door would be a strange-looking, middle-aged lady wearing a lot of make-up, called Fleur.

***

It's hard to know, even in retrospect, who was the most surprised. As the two men at the bar turned towards him, PC Crocker saw his Chief Superintendent sitting alongside the man whom he had last seen, completely naked, strung up, swinging from the ceiling, and who was now sitting on a bar stool on which there was a plump cushion.

Crocker's jaw once again locked into its open monosyllabic position. 'Ah,' he managed to articulate. He was in no doubt that sitting just a couple of yards away from him was his boss, but he was dressed strangely. Crocker had never seen the Chief Super out of uniform, and yet here he now was, apparently dressed as a cowboy. He was wearing brown boots with Cuban heels, jeans, a pair of leather chaps and a checked waistcoat over an open-necked frilly shirt.

The Chief Super coughed. 'Is that you, Crocker?'

'Yes, sir.'

'Good God, man, you look awful.'

'Thank you, sir.'

The Chief looked about the room and coughed again. 'Thought I'd do a bit of undercover work myself, Crocker. See how you were getting on.'

'That's very thoughtful of you, sir.'

'Well, how are you getting on?'

'Very well, thank you, sir.'

'Have you discovered who the murderer is yet?'

Crocker, now well outside his comfort zone and completely unable to keep up with events, reverted to his original theory.

'I think you're sitting next to him, sir.'

'What d'you mean? Don't be an ass, man. This is Billy Bishop, an old friend.' The Chief Super paused for a moment, as if realising that what he had said might later prove incriminating. 'Well, not really an old friend; in fact, I've only just met him, but he's a pillar of society.'

'That's as maybe, sir, but I saw him earlier. He was tied up and one of the residents was caning him in order to force him to admit that he was the killer.' Now all three around the bar looked at Crocker in complete amazement. Ivy, the Chief and Bill Bishop stared at Crocker in utter disbelief.

Crocker, mistaking their expression of incredulity for one of admiration, now became more confident and continued, 'D'you want me to arrest him now, sir, or should I wait until I put in my formal written report tomorrow?'

On hearing this, the Chief's eyes widened. 'Ah, well, Crocker, let's not be too hasty. You've done a great job, but I think you may have been undercover a bit too long. You may have been overdoing it.'

'How d'you mean, sir?'

'Ah, well... ah... getting the wrong end of the stick as it were.'

After wriggling uncomfortably on his cushioned stool for a moment, the man who had been tied up and punished joined in the conversation. 'If I were you, lad, I'd keep shtum about this 'ole episode.'

Crocker, who was still in a state of partial catatonia, didn't register what the Yorkshireman had said and continued undeterred. 'You've got to hand it to Ivy and her residents, sir. They obviously knew all along who the killer was, so they lured him in here, strung him up, got a confession and, hey presto, Bob's your uncle, here he is!' Crocker finished his little speech triumphantly and pointed at the man sitting on the cushion.

Once more, all three looked at Crocker aghast. It was the Chief who responded first. 'Crocker, you've gone mad. Why don't you get a good night's sleep and come along to the station tomorrow? In the meantime, it might be best if you didn't mention any of this,' and the Chief indicated his costume, 'to anyone, as it, ah, might blow my cover.'

'Yes, sir.'

'Might also be best not to mention that you saw this man, the Labour candidate, whom I've never met before, either.'

'Absolutely, whatever you say, sir.'

'I suspect you're not regular, Crocker. That's usually the problem in situations like this. By the way, any news on the stolen bicycle?'

'The one with drop handlebars and pink mudguards?'

'Yes, that's the one.'

'Not since a reported sighting last autumn, sir.'

'Well, keep alert and stay regular. What must you do?'

'Keep alert and stay regular, sir.'

'That's good. Now, off you pop and I'll see you tomorrow.'

EIGHTEEN

The following morning, Crocker once again slipped out of the guesthouse early, carrying his disguise in a plastic bag. He had not slept well and was beginning to think that maybe the Chief had been right: he'd gone mad. All sorts of ridiculous thoughts flooded into his consciousness. Maybe where he was staying wasn't a guesthouse at all. Maybe it was one of those houses where women meet men, a... he could barely bring himself to think the word, let alone say it – a bordello. Maybe the nurse wasn't really a qualified nurse, and as for the chambermaid, well, she certainly worked odd hours. Then there was the half-German, half-French, half-English, Parisian girl who had obtained the confession. Surely they weren't – well – *'you knows'*, thought Crocker.

Then what was the Chief Super doing dressed up as a cowboy? Certainly it was nice of him to be concerned about one of his men and to come to see how he, Crocker, was getting on with his investigation, but a cowboy costume was hardly the most appropriate disguise. It was a basic rule of undercover work that you needed to blend in, not stand out. To be indistinguishable from the man, or indeed in his own case the woman, in the street – a cowboy in Clapham was hardly going to go unnoticed. Then, most confusing of all was the man from Yorkshire. If he was the murderer, then what was he doing chatting to the Chief Superintendent? If he wasn't, then what on earth was he doing swinging totally naked from the ceiling of the guesthouse in a rope net and being punished by the part-French, part-German, part-English, Parisian girl; and, for heaven's sake, what was he being punished *for*?

Crocker decided to go to the police station early to prepare his report before his meeting with the Chief. Later that morning at the appointed time he approached the desk sergeant, gave him a copy of his report and said, 'Morning, Sarge, the boss is expecting me.'

'Rather you than me, Crocker; he was in a foul mood when he arrived first thing, I can tell you. Go straight in. He's waiting for you.'

Crocker tightened his tie, took a deep breath, walked smartly to the door of the Chief's office and knocked.

'Come,' came a disembodied voice from inside. Crocker entered and stood to attention in front of the Chief who, once again resplendent in his neatly pressed uniform, was sitting behind his desk.

'Sit down, Crocker,' began the Chief.

'Thank you, sir.'

'Now, about last night.'

'Yes, sir, what about last night?'

'I think it might be best if we kept the events of last night between ourselves.'

'Couldn't agree with you more, sir. The fewer people who know about the strange occurrences of last night, the better.'

'I'm glad we see eye to eye on that.' The Chief seemed to be relieved.

'And that is exactly what I've said in my report, a copy of which I have brought with me, sir.'

'Ah! Your report – yes.' The Chief looked alarmed. 'There are other copies, you say?' he asked with an attempt at nonchalance.

'I followed procedure, sir. I have left a copy with the desk sergeant and have kept one for my own records.'

The Chief then resumed his usual gruff tone. 'Well, to be honest, Crocker, I'm not sure anyone will believe what you have to say. I've been worried about you, Crocker. I think you may have gone mad.'

'I was beginning to wonder as well, sir, but I think I'm beginning to understand what is going on in the guesthouse – and it's not all it seems.'

'Ah.' The Chief Super coughed. 'And what do you mean by that?'

'Well, sir, it may seem ridiculous to you, but I'm beginning to think it might be a...,' Crocker hesitated before saying under his breath, 'a brothel.'

'A what? I can't hear you, man. Speak up,' blustered the Chief.

'A brothel, a bordello, a house of ill-repute, sir.'

'A brothel? Nonsense. Have you lost your mind, man? What d'you think I would be doing in a brothel with that charming lady, Ivy? Are you calling me a brothel-creeper, Crocker?'

'No, no, sir, of course not. You, like me, were undercover.'

'Mmm.'

'But the man you were with, the Labour candidate, I'm confused by his behaviour. I'm no longer sure if he is the murderer.'

'Of course he's not; Crusher Ericsson is. Look, Crocker, you've been overdoing it and I think you've lost your mind. I'm going to pull you off this case before you become terminally insane.'

'But I've still not achieved my goal of identifying the killer, sir.'

'Never mind that. Now leave your report with me and go home. I think you should take the next week off. Come back after the by-election. I don't want you to go back to the bro—' The Chief coughed. 'Er, the guesthouse ever again. Brothel, indeed; that's outrageous! Now off you go and if I were you I'd take a laxative. That's your problem, Crocker, not regular enough.'

'Certainly, sir.'

'Okay, off you go straight home and no more undercover work, d'you hear?'

'Yes, sir.'

Crocker saluted smartly and the Chief accompanied him to the door. As Crocker marched out of the office, the Chief observed the desk sergeant, a file open on the desk in front of him, look up at him and smile.

Back at his flat, PC Crocker sat down, stroked his cat and initially felt a sense of relief that he had been taken off the case. He began to think that the intense strain of working undercover was beginning to affect his judgement adversely. The Chief was right, he thought: much more of this and he might go permanently mad. But then he felt a sense of unease. He had not completed his mission. He had not discovered who killed poor Rosie Little. The residents, or whatever they were, of the guesthouse, or whatever it was, were depending on him to remove that menace from society, and he could not let them down. Then there was Crusher Ericsson, a hard man with a soft centre, who would be waiting for him – well, for his alter-ego, Fleur – that night.

Crocker had never disobeyed an order in his life before, but he now knew what he had to do. He had to return to the guesthouse one last time and see if he could discover whether or not Crusher was the killer. He fed his cat, donned his disguise and in the late afternoon once more set out for the guesthouse.

***

Lucinda was tired, fed up and wanted a drink. She'd had a dismal afternoon canvassing on behalf of Andy

Norris. True, the reduced alcohol tax was well-received by some of those who had deigned to speak to her, but no one had heard of the BAD Party, and she was disconsolate as she walked to the hostelry where she was to meet Andy and Lucy. As she was walking past the discreet entrance to a guesthouse, she realised that she had one leaflet left and decided that this would be her last call of the day.

Lucinda knocked on the door and was slightly taken aback when the door was opened by a rather plain, middle-aged lady with long blonde hair who was wearing a thick layer of brightly coloured make-up. 'Good evening,' said Lucinda. 'Are you the proprietress of this establishment?'

Crocker, for it was he who had answered the door, replied that the owner of the guesthouse was busy with her clients, but could he, that is she, be of any assistance?

'I'm canvassing on behalf of the BAD Party,' Lucinda boomed. 'Mr Norris is the candidate to vote for. Will you be voting for him, madam?' enquired Lucinda.

Crocker thought for a moment, before realising why he recognised the name. 'Ah, yes! I heard he was standing. I know him from a previous case.'

'Case?'

'I mean, campaign.'

'Good, good.' This was by far the most promising doorstep discussion she had engaged in all afternoon.

'Perhaps I can have a word with you then?' – and Lucinda, without waiting for an answer, walked past Crocker and into the hallway.

Crocker, slightly wrong-footed by Lucinda's actions, ushered her into the front room, where a few tradesmen had already congregated about the bar. She registered with some surprise that there was a nurse and a chambermaid at the bar, standing alongside a man she vaguely recognised.

Lucinda and PC Crocker took a seat at one of the tables, where they exchanged pleasantries for a moment before Crocker asked how the campaign was going.

'Well, Fleur, if I may call you that, Andrew – that is Mr Norris – as you will know from working with him in the past, is an outstanding candidate. He is exactly what Clarmers need to represent them on the council.'

'Clarmers?' asked Fleur, not understanding.

'Oh, you probably know them as people from Clapham.'

'Ah, Clapham Commoners.'

'Precisely.'

Fleur looked at Lucinda questioningly, as his own memory of Norris was one of an aimless and rather vacuous man whose only interests were beer and darts.

'The reason Norris is so suitable,' Lucinda continued, 'is that he's never had an original thought in his life and will not do anything stupid and try to change anything. You know, all that nonsense about improving society? Equality: all that kind of rubbish. No, he will work tirelessly for the *status quo*, stagnating in County Hall until the next election. No boats rocked, no promises broken, no policies – so no U-turns. Without a doubt he's the man for us. Will you vote for him?'

PC Crocker thought for a moment. 'Well, in these uncertain times it would be reassuring to know that one candidate at least will have no effect whatsoever on the constituency. Yes, I'm impressed.'

'Fleur, you're brilliant! I'll put you down as a supporter.' Lucinda didn't think it necessary to add that she was the first of the afternoon. 'By the way, who's that man at the bar? I think I recognise him.'

PC Crocker looked at the man Lucinda had indicated. 'Oh, that's Bill Bishop, the Labour candidate.'

'Oh, is it now?' Lucinda allowed a smile to cross her face briefly.

'Yes, he was here last night, but then he was swinging naked from a net attached to the ceiling and being caned by a French girl.'

'Was he indeed?'

'Yes. I'm sure you'll have a lot in common, both being involved with the by-election. Let me introduce you. Of course, he's well ahead in the polls.'

'Is he now? Maybe I can do something about that.'

Fleur then guided Lucinda across the room to where Bill Bishop was sitting at the bar. 'Bill,' he said, 'I'd like to introduce you to someone who is canvassing for the BAD Party.'

Bill turned around, and on recognising Crocker, his eyes widened with astonishment. 'But I was told you wouldn't be back.' Then his gaze turned to the refined-looking lady who was standing next to Crocker, dressed as though she was about to go for a brisk walk on the moor.

'Mr Bishop,' she said, smiling sweetly. 'How nice to meet you. Let me introduce myself.'

It was at that moment that Crocker, alias Fleur, noticed Crusher, alias Jeremy, enter the bar, once again carrying a bunch of flowers. 'Excuse me,' he said to Lucinda, 'I'll have to go,' and he turned to meet Crusher, who presented his flowers and kissed Crocker on the cheek.

'Hello, Jeremy,' Crocker said, attempting a smile.

'Hello, Fleur, it's good to see you.' Crusher hesitated for a moment. 'I've made a decision, Fleur. I want you to be my confidante.' Crusher seemed uneasy and Crocker was unsettled. He was worried that Crusher might have meant something other than confidante.

'Fleur, I need to talk to you – in private.'

Crocker was becoming more and more nervous about Crusher's intentions. 'B-but, Jeremy, you know I haven't made up my mind.'

'I know, Fleur. Have a glass of wine. Red or white?'

'Red, please.'

That's what I like about you, Fleur, you've got class.' He turned to the bar and shouted, 'Ivy! Two glasses of red.'

Drinks in hand, Crusher resumed his conversation. 'Fleur, I've got something to say to you and I need all of your attention. We need to go upstairs. I need privacy for what I'm going to do.'

Crocker gulped and made an attempt to lift his glass of wine, but he was shaking so much that he spilt most of it over Crusher's shirt, leaving a deep red stain. 'Fleur, you're shaking,' he said.

'Sorry, Jeremy, this is all so sudden; I don't seem to know what's going on any more. I'm a nervous wreck.'

'Just stay there, Fleur. I'll get us a room.'

Crocker's eyes widened and his legs wobbled as Crusher went to the bar and spoke to Ivy. 'Room 21,' she said, handing him a key, and, as Crusher returned to Fleur's side, Ivy left the bar and walked rapidly to her office, picked up the phone and dialled a number. After what seemed to her to be an interminable delay, her call was answered. 'Cecil,' she said, 'you need to get over here urgently. All hell's going to break loose soon.' Then, after a pause while she listened, she added, 'No, don't bother, just come as you are.'

Back in the bar, Lucinda was beginning to make her way to the exit, leaving Bill Bishop looking very pale sitting at the bar, while Crusher grabbed Crocker's hand, saying, 'Fleur, come with me, I know what I've got to do,' and led him gently out of the bar and up the stairs to Room 21.

NINETEEN

'Andrew, I think I have just increased your chances of getting elected a hundredfold.'

'I expected you to be a good canvasser, Lucinda, but 'ow 'ave you managed to do that?' Lucy looked across the table at her friend. The three of them were in the Plough, a pub on the Common, sharing their experiences of the afternoon over a drink.

'Well, Andrew, let's just say that the Labour candidate may not be standing any more.'

'You haven't killed him, have you?' Andy asked, aghast.

'Don't be silly; of course not.'

'But you said you wanted to neutralise him.'

'I think he may have just neutralised himself.' Lucinda took a sip of wine. 'I can't say any more, but I think I may have persuaded him that it would be in the best interests of Clapham society in general, and the BAD Party in particular, if he were to stand down as a candidate in the by-election.' Lucinda put her glass back on the table, a broad smile of satisfaction written all across her face. 'What a *nasty* little man. Now, Andrew, we must start working on your speech for the hustings next week.'

Meanwhile, up in Room 21, PC Crocker was shaking. Shaking uncontrollably with fear. He was sitting primly on the edge of a red, velvet-covered settee which was placed close to a double bed in a dimly-lit, seductively-furnished boudoir. In his lap, clutched firmly with both hands, was a small, red, shiny plastic handbag. Below the hem of his short skirt, his stockinged legs were visible, splayed in a rather unladylike fashion, while his knees, which could only be described as knobbly, were visibly shaking.

It was stiflingly hot in the bedroom and drips of sweat trickled from PC Crocker's underarms on to his bra, which contained dusters now damp and uncomfortable. His wig was itchy and he had to resist the temptation to scratch his scalp, and he suspected his make-up was beginning to run. He tried to think, but couldn't. He was aware that in dangerous situations like this a cool, calm head and ice-cold reasoning were essential; but, try as he might, all he could do was shake and whimper while random images of what possible unpleasantness might be perpetrated on him flashed across his mind, making him incapable of formulating any cogent strategy. He knew that any second now the game would be up and his cover blown. As soon as Crusher, who was currently in the bathroom next door washing himself, discovered his true identity, he, PC Crocker, was as good as dead. Odd, seemingly random thoughts once more shot through his mind like firecrackers exploding on a dark night. 'I'm going to die, be murdered like Rosie,' he thought to himself. He could now hear Crusher urinating noisily. 'When he finds out I'm a man, he'll kill me,' thought the policeman. Then Crocker considered, 'Maybe he's a homosexual. Oh *no*, that would be even worse. How on earth have I managed to get myself into this mess?' he pondered. Then it occurred to him how ironic it was that although throughout his whole life he had been chronically unable to attract a member of the opposite sex, it appeared that he had now endeared himself to another man. 'How on earth hasn't he realised that I'm a man?' he said out loud. Crocker began to hyperventilate and became slightly dizzy. 'Calm down. Calm down,' he said to himself. 'Remember your training.'

Crocker took a couple of deep breaths and began to search in the little bag for something useful to defend himself with, but all he could find was the advert for a firm of dry cleaners and a tampon. He looked wistfully at the locked bedroom door and it was then that he heard the toilet flush and the door of the en-suite bathroom opened. From within emerged Crusher, alias Jeremy Small, naked from the waist up. 'I've left my shirt soaking in the sink,' he said as he walked over to where Crocker was seated.

Crusher looked at the luckless policeman seated nervously on the edge of the settee. 'Now, Fleur, I think you know why I've brought you here,' he said as he advanced across the room to where PC Crocker sat whimpering while nervously fingering his handbag. Crusher knelt down in front of Crocker and put his head in the policeman's lap. 'Fleur,' he said, 'you've made me realise what a good woman can do for a man. Made me realise that you don't have to be tough all the time. You see, I was laughed at when I was a child because my name was Jeremy Small. The other kids used to say that I had a small willy. Then, suddenly one day I lost my temper and I hit one of the other boys. I hurt him and was sent to Borstal as a result. When I was let out, I changed my name to Crusher Ericsson. No one would mess with a man called Crusher Ericsson, I thought – and I was right: no one has messed with me since.'

Crocker remained perfectly still, not wanting to interrupt Crusher's soliloquy. He wondered what Crusher would do next. What was he leading up to? Would he want to seduce him? Crocker went cold at the thought.

'Anyway,' continued Crusher, 'since then I've made a living from crushing people for money. You know: bouncer, bodyguard, that sort of thing. But the thing is, Fleur, I didn't mean to kill her.' Suddenly, Crocker went rigid. 'There! I've said it,' continued Crusher. 'I didn't mean to kill Rosie; I liked her a lot. You see, I just knew her as Rosie. I was taking her out for a meal when I asked her what her surname was and she said it was Little. I totally misunderstood what she meant; I didn't realise that her name really was Rosie Little. Suddenly, it all came back to me. Being called Jeremy Small and all the verbal abuse I received and the insinuations about the size of my willy. I thought she was taking the piss out of me. I lost my temper; I didn't mean to kill her. I don't remember much about it, to be honest, but I must have pushed her and she fell, hitting her head. I knew that with my record I would be accused of murder, so I hid the body under a nearby bush and kept quiet.' Crocker could hear Crusher sobbing quietly at the memory. 'Then you came along.'

Crocker's face, luckily invisible to Crusher, was a picture of absolute terror. His eyes were wide, his mouth wide open and dribbling. For the third time in as many days, he was in a state of total mental collapse. He didn't dare move a muscle or say a word. His head ached with the random thoughts that whirled around his brain. Disconnected images momentarily splashed on to his cerebrum like a stroboscope in a dance hall. How on earth was he going to get out of this mess alive? Was Crusher confessing to him before he himself was to be killed? Did Crusher still have a crush on him? Whatever happened to the stolen bicycle? Was Crusher a psychopathic mass murderer, or a gentle giant with a small willy? The man whose head was in his lap was now silent apart from the sound of gentle sobbing. Crocker felt there was a need to say something: to respond in some way to Crusher's momentous confession. Eventually, he muttered, 'Ah.'

'Pardon?' said Crusher, lifting his head from Crocker's lap and looking up into his face.

'I just said, "Ah".'

'Oh.' Crusher dabbed his eyes with Crocker's skirt. 'You see, Fleur, in you I saw goodness and honesty, the attributes I had lost when I changed from Jeremy to Crusher. Even your name is sweet and fragrant, and you seemed to me to be the perfect woman, the girlfriend I never had, the mother that died young. Here, I thought, is someone I can confess to. Then, in the knowledge that you will always be there for me, I can repay my debt to society, and when I come out there you'll be, waiting for me.' At this point, Crocker began to hyperventilate again as Crusher continued, 'You will wait for me, won't you, Fleur?'

Crocker knew an answer was required, and that answer needed to be in the affirmative, but the words stuck in his throat. 'You will wait for me, won't you?' Crusher pleaded, then even more urgently, 'however long it is.'

Crocker's throat was dry and all he could articulate was, 'Uh.'

Luckily, just then there came a knock on the door. 'Are you in there, Crocker?'

He recognised the Chief Super's voice and realised that any moment his cover would be blown and Crusher would know not only that he was a man, but a policeman to boot. 'No,' he shouted, 'there's no PC Crocker in here, just me: Fleur, with Jeremy.'

'Oh! Awfully sorry. Must have got the wrong room,' came the reply. Crocker now began to panic as his timely salvation appeared to be slipping away; but luckily the Chief realised his mistake just in time. 'Oh yes, of course it's you, Fleur. May Ivy and I come in, please?'

'Jeremy,' Crocker said, 'the man at the door is a policeman and you can give yourself up to him. Tell him what you told me.'

'Thank you, Fleur. You think of everything.'

Crocker gently removed Jeremy's head from his lap, went to the door and unlocked it. There, on the landing, stood the Chief and Ivy. 'Come in,' he said. 'This is Jeremy Little. He has confessed to me.'

'What d'you mean, Crock— I mean Fleur? Are you a bloody priest now?'

'He has confessed to the unintentional killing of one Rosie Little, formerly of this establishment. He is willing to go to the police station and give a statement to that effect.'

The Chief Super entered the room and looked at the half-naked man sitting on the floor, his eyes red with tears. 'Is that true, Mr Ericsson?'

'It's Mr Small, and yes, it is true. I killed Rosie, but it was an accident, after a misunderstanding – she fell.'

The Chief then formally cautioned Jeremy Small and was about to cuff him when he realised that in his rush he had not brought his pair of handcuffs. 'Crock— urm, Fleur, do you have your 'cuffs on you?'

'Why on earth should I be carrying handcuffs?' Crocker looked at the Chief, his eyes wide and appealing.

'Of course not,' added the Chief quickly, 'no reason at all. It's not as if you're a policeman in disguise, or anything like that.'

'I think I might be able to lay my hands on a pair,' said Ivy quietly.

A few minutes later, securely cuffed, Crusher, alias Jeremy, was led away to a Black Maria which the Chief had summoned. As he stepped into the van, his last words were to Crocker, 'You *will* wait for me, Fleur, won't you?'

Relief was written all over Crocker's face. 'Of course I will, Jeremy,' he said.

***

Andy was reading the *Evening News*, a half-full pint of lager on the table in front of him. 'I see they've caught the killer of that girl on Clapham Common, Zeph. *And*,' Andy looked at his friend, 'it *wasn't* me.'

'I bet you had somethin' to do with it.'

'No, not at all. Look, a man called Jeremy Small has been charged with her murder.'

Andy turned the page and after a moment he groaned out loud, '*Oh no!*'

'What's the matter, man? You sound like you've seen a ghost.'

'You'll never believe it, Zeph.'

'Believe what, man?'

'The Labour candidate has resigned!'

'What d'you mean, man?'

Andy read out loud. "Mr Bill Bishop, the Labour candidate in the Clapham Common by-election, has announced that he will be withdrawing from the election for personal reasons. In an interview he said that he wanted to spend more time with his family."'

'Hey, man, that's the poll leader who's quit.' Zephaniah began to laugh. 'Hey, you might jus' get elected!'

'Don't say that, Zeph. This is a nightmare.'

'But you wanted to run the country, or at least Clapham Common. Now maybe you will!'

'No, Zeph, I just wanted to impress Lucy, make her think that there was more to me than beer and darts.'

'And it's worked. You said she's all over you now.'

'Yes, but I don't want to get elected; it would interfere too much with my lifestyle.'

'Don' worry, man, there's still that Liberal candidate. He's miles ahead of you – he'll win. Even that Martian man will probably get more votes than you.'

'Yes, you're right. I just need to put in a good performance at the hustings, impress Lucy with my magnanimous losing speech when the weedy Liberal wins a week on Thursday, and then it will all be over.

Yeah, no problem, nothing can go wrong. Another drink, Zeph?'

TWENTY

The Chief Superintendent was reflecting on his fortunes, or rather lack of them. Seated behind his desk, he gazed at the photograph of his passing-out parade on the wall beside him. 'Chief Constable, Sir Cecil Winterbottom' had such a ring to it, and for a moment it had seemed possible. However, with the untimely withdrawal of Bill Bishop from the electoral race, all hope of promotion and a knighthood had suddenly evaporated. If Crocker had only obeyed orders, Bishop might have got away with it. And, the Chief realised, it had been a close call for him as well. If it hadn't been for a bit of quick thinking on his part, something he wasn't renowned for, he might have been in a spot of trouble himself. 'It's a good job Crocker is so naïve,' he said to himself. It was fortunate that he had managed to convince Crocker that he, too, was undercover that evening, but Bill had paid the price. He, the Chief Super, had warned him to stay away from the guesthouse and the French girl until after the election, but the Labour candidate had been over-confident. 'Once elected, you can do what you want,' he'd said to him. 'You can swing from the beams in the bloody House of Commons if you want – plenty of others do – but wait till you've been elected.' But Bill was arrogant, thought he couldn't be damaged by an insignificant minnow like Crocker. Nor had Bill considered that influential men, or in this case a woman, might just be supporting one of his opponents. 'Ah.' The Chief Super sighed at the lost opportunity. 'Never mind, at least I've caught Rosie Little's murderer.' Indeed, since he had announced the arrest and subsequent confession of a man for the Clapham Common murder, as it had become known, the press had heaped praise on him and his force. 'As for Crocker,' the Chief thought to himself, 'that imbecile nearly wrecked everything, but somehow he did manage to wheedle a confession out of one of the most dangerous men in Clapham.' His thoughts were interrupted by a knock on the door. 'Come,' he shouted, and the door opened to admit PC Crocker, who was dressed smartly in his uniform.

'Ah, Crocker, come and sit down.' As Crocker advanced into the room, the Chief swivelled his chair and ended up facing the opposite corner of his office. 'Where are you, man?' he shouted, confused.

'I'm over here, sir, behind you.'

The Chief swivelled back and, feeling slightly giddy, said, 'Ah, there you are. Do keep still, man.' After a moment to allow his dizziness to settle, he continued, 'Now, Crocker, I want you to know that I'm not pleased that you disobeyed orders. I told you not to go back to the bordello... er... guesthouse, didn't I?'

'Yes, sir.'

'And what did you do?'

'I went back, sir.'

'Yes, you went back, against my explicit instructions.'

'Yes, sir, but I just wanted one more opportunity to nail the killer, sir.'

'That's a disciplinary offence, you know.'

'What, nailing murderers, sir?'

'No, you idiot, going back to bordellos..., oh blast: *guesthouses*, when you've specifically been told not to.'

'Yes, sir. Sorry, sir.'

'You've put me in a very difficult position, Crocker.'

'Sorry, sir.'

The Chief paused for a moment as though deep in thought. 'But I'm willing to overlook it on this occasion.'

'Oh, thank you, sir.'

'On one condition.'

'And what is that?'

'That you keep quiet about my little undercover escapade.'

'But I thought you were very good, sir. Maybe the cowboy outfit was a little obvious as there are relatively few cowboys around Clapham, but in my opinion the disguise was excellent.'

'The fewer people who know about that the better.' The Chief cleared his throat noisily. 'I might need to use that disguise again – not to go to the broth... er, guesthouse obviously, but on some future unrelated case. D'you understand?'

'Absolutely, sir.'

'Good.'

'Now, about that man Bishop. Funny sort of cove, not that I'd met him before that night when you saw us together. Funny how he managed to accidentally get caught up in a net with no clothes on. Probably best not to mention that either, Crocker.'

'Absolutely, sir. I suspect he wasn't regular.'

'That's probably true, Crocker. I think you're beginning to understand the importance of regularity.' The Chief peered intently at his PC. 'How are you on the old peristaltic front?'

'Fine, thank you, sir.'

'Well, that's enough about the strange events in the guesthouse. The important thing is that, with Crusher's confession, we can close the file on the Clapham Common murder.'

'Jeremy, sir.'

'What d'you mean, Jeremy?'

'Jeremy, sir, that's his name.'

'Oh, whatever. He's a nasty piece of work – that's for sure. You'll need to watch yourself when he gets out, but that shouldn't be for twenty years or more.'

'He's just misunderstood, sir. I would like to put a word in on his behalf.'

'Rubbish, man. He deserves to go down for life.'

'But it was an accident, sir. Rosie Little fell and hit her head.'

'Crocker, sometimes I wonder about you. No, you may *not* appear as a character witness for his defence.'

Crocker hesitated for a moment. 'Talking of files, sir, I wonder if you've had a chance to read my report yet.'

'What report?'

'The report I made describing the events of the evening when you went undercover as a cowboy, and I discovered that the Labour candidate had somehow managed to fall into a net while stark naked.'

'Ah, no. I seem to have mislaid it.'

'Well, the sergeant has got a copy. Shall I get it for you?'

'Er – that seems to have been mislaid as well.'

'Gosh, then it's a good job I have my copy, sir, isn't it?' Crocker smiled innocently at the Chief, who cleared his throat loudly.

'Ah, um, I suppose, under the circumstances, you could say a word or two in Crusher's—'

'Jeremy's.'

'Ah, yes, Jeremy's favour.'

'Thank you, sir.'

TWENTY-ONE

'I'm evva so proud of you, Andy,' Lucy said as she straightened his tie. 'There, that's better.'

'Thanks, Lucy, I'd better be off.'

'Lucinda and Rupert said they'd meet me at the hall, so good luck.' Lucy gave Andy a peck on the cheek and then a small hug. 'I'll see you afterwards.'

It was the night of the hustings, and Andy set off to the town hall in a jaunty frame of mind. He had definitely turned the situation around with Lucy. Although he hadn't actually asked her out, she had been very supportive, even affectionate, towards him over the last week or so, and his ruse to impress her looked as though it would eventually bring home the proverbial bacon. A good speech tonight, he thought, then lose the election next week and that should be that – in the bag. Of course, in order to get the maximum sympathy from Lucy he'd have to remember to be totally inconsolable about losing. A few phrases along the lines of: 'I really wanted to do something to help society,' and, 'This was a real opportunity for me *and* for Clapham.' Or, 'This could have been the making of me, a chance to *do* something with my life' would do the trick. He particularly liked the last lament, as it sounded selfless yet sincere. However, before rehearsing his losing speech, he needed to perform sufficiently well at the hustings to give the impression that he really believed he could win and actually wanted to. He had studied a few speeches made by politicians and some film stars, and patched together a few phrases which he thought were rousing yet had the right amount of *gravitas*.

The Town Hall smelt musty, as such places always do, and the noise of spindly chairs being scraped on wooden flooring echoed in the half-full hall. About fifty members of the general public were dotted around the room, while fast asleep in the front row was a man whose badge proclaimed him to be a member of the Press. The seats near him were vacant, possibly because of the strong smell of alcohol in the immediate vicinity.

On the stage were three seats and a lectern, at which the chairman, a local dignitary, was arranging some papers. He introduced himself to Andy. 'Look, Mr Norris, let's keep this short,' he said. 'We all know who's going to win, so there's no point in prolonging the agony. I need to be in the Coach and Horses by eight. All right?'

'Suits me,' replied Andy, who was beginning to feel rather nervous. 'Where are the others?'

'Well, the Martian candidate has left a message to say that he cannot be present in person, but will be communing with us from above the stratosphere – whatever that means. He's clearly mad – and the Liberal candidate hasn't arrived yet.' The chairman looked up and saw an elderly-looking man walking across the room towards the stage. 'Ah, here he is. Right! Let's get started.'

The Liberal candidate had a wispy beard and was wearing a thick woolly jumper and brown corduroy trousers. He had forgotten to take off his cycle clips and was carrying a plastic carrier bag which appeared to contain his shopping. 'Sorry I'm late,' he said to the chairman, and then gave Andy a limp, moist handshake. Andy thought the man was so unprepossessing that no one could possibly vote for him, and once more began to worry that he might conceivably win this electoral contest. He made a mental note to make sure that Zephaniah and Ted voted either Liberal or Martian. He then reassured himself with the thought that the Liberal had hundreds if not thousands of supporters, while he, Andy, had only five. There could be no doubt about the outcome.

After calling the meeting to order, the chairman invited the Liberal candidate to deliver his opening remarks. The weedy man, still wearing his bicycle clips, spoke in a low, monotonous tone that was barely audible. Even Andy, who was sitting right beside him, couldn't hear what he was saying, while those in the audience also had to contend with the ever-increasing volume of snoring from the journalist in the front row.

It was then Andy's turn. He decided to give it everything. 'My lords,' he began (conscious that Rupert was in the audience), 'ladies and gentlemen.' His tone was low and sonorous. 'I have decided that enough is enough.' He paused for effect, looking around the room as though assessing whether his audience was keeping up with his rhetoric, before continuing, 'It is time to put my head on the block of destiny, to gaze over the parapet of the future, to seek a vision – even if it gets shot off.' Once more Andy gazed around the half-full hall, before continuing in a louder voice, 'Yes, ladies and gentlemen, a vision – a vision of Clapham, but not the one I see before me now: it is a vision of a bigger, better, brighter Clapham.' He glanced at Lucy, who was looking at him, her eyes wide with admiration. Next to her, both Lucinda and Rupert were fast asleep. 'I have decided that Clapham needs a vision, not just for now but from Birth to Death.' Here Lucy started to clap, then, realising that no one else was, stopped and hid her face in embarrassment. Andy then delivered what he considered to be his best line. 'Don't ask what Clapham can do for *you*: ask what you can do for *Clapham.*' He knew he had heard this somewhere before and thought it suited the occasion rather well. He continued in the same strident Churchillian tones, 'I have asked that question – and I know the answer. What *is* the answer?' It was at this moment that Andy lost his concentration, as can happen to even the greatest of orators. He repeated his last sentence, hoping that his memory would return. 'What is the answer? Well, I'll tell you what the answer is, it is...' He paused – his mind a complete blank. He tried to pretend that it was a pregnant pause. '*I'll* tell you what it is.' His voice now thundered with passion. 'I'll *tell* you what it is...' A few members of the audience were now looking at Andy, urging him on to tell them the answer, even though most had forgotten the question. Andy had now totally lost the thread of his speech, so he did the only thing possible under the circumstances – he pointed to the ceiling and started shouting. 'I'll tell you: I said I'll do everything I can for Clapham. It's either me or the borough – *one of us must go.*' Andy now dropped his voice almost to a whisper. 'So, ladies and gentlemen, that – *that* is why I've decided to stand. This borough is rotten; if you want it pruned and made healthy, you need a gardener. *I* am that gardener. Vote for the Birth and Death Party.' Andy stopped, thinking that this would be a good place to finish, and there was complete silence in the room apart from the sound of snoring coming from the front row; but as he sat down, a polite ripple of applause ran around the room and, for a moment, even the snoring ceased.

Now those readers who know a thing or two about politics will have spotted that Andy's speech was a little light on facts or policy, but that didn't matter; all that mattered was that Lucy was clapping enthusiastically. The chairman, after looking at his watch and realising it was nearly seven thirty, declared that there was no time for questions and closed the meeting.

Half an hour later, settled with their drinks at a table in the Plough, Andy was being congratulated by his supporters. 'You were great, Andy. All that stuff about parapets and getting your head blown off, that was brilliant, that was.' Lucy was beaming.

'Thanks, Lucy,' Andy said. 'I did my best. It's quite easy to be a great orator if you feel passionate about something. Now, I just need the mandate to deliver.'

'You were very good, Andrew, I think you'll make a great politician. You spoke for nearly half an hour and managed to say absolutely nothing. There was no substance to your speech at all, yet one felt roused by it. You've a natural talent.' Lucinda took a sip from her gin and tonic.

'That other chap, the Liberal, I couldn't hear a word of what he was saying. He seemed to be snoring,' Rupert added.

'Well, Andrew, it's now a two-horse race, the BADs against the Libs.' Lucinda took a sip of her drink, then continued, 'I fear the latter will still win, but there's no doubt that on tonight's performance you deserve the seat.'

'Oh, Lucinda, don't talk like that. Andy can still win, can't you, Andy?' Lucy looked pleadingly at her housemate.

'It won't be easy, Lucy, but you can be sure I'll give it my best shot. I'll fight with every last breath in my body, until there's no breath or body left, and if I don't win, it will not be for want of breath, or body.'

Lucinda and Rupert looked at Andy, bemused. 'Quite,' said Lucinda. 'Think positive, Andrew. We've still a week of canvassing to turn this around. Lucy, dear, you are absolutely right. We *can* do it. I'm going to get on to Ponsonby what's-his-name, now that he's fully recovered, and we'll get him to campaign on your behalf. He and his cronies might just be enough to tip the balance in your favour.'

An expression of alarm momentarily flitted across Andy's face. 'Oh, I wouldn't want to trouble him.'

'But it was his resignation that triggered this by-election and is the reason we're in this mess, Andrew. That and the fact you shot him in the backside.'

'I could have a word with a few pals at the club. You never know: there may be a few strings I can pull there,' added Rupert.

Alarm registered again on Andy's face. 'I really wouldn't want to put you to any trouble, Rupert.'

'Dear boy, it's no problem at all. We *need* you, Andy. You'd be perfect. Your ability to be convincing without committing yourself to anything whatsoever, is nothing short of astonishing. You're a natural. By the way, where's your chairman?'

'Yeah, and your agent?' added Lucy.

Andy panicked. He hadn't told Lucy that Zephaniah and Ted were his two party officials. 'Sadly busy canvassing tonight. It's almost impossible to get them to take time off, they're so committed.'

And so, Andy and his BAD Party entered the final week of the by-election campaign.

One way and another, it was a busy week for the BAD candidate. Daily meetings with his agent in the Herald Lounge Bar were immediately followed by briefings with his chairman in the Nell Gwyn. The pressure of the campaign was beginning to take its toll, and Andy was quite exhausted by the time polling day arrived.

TWENTY-TWO

It was polling day, and that evening PC Crocker was on duty at the polling station. He was pleased to be back in uniform, comfortable in the knowledge that, with his helmet and dark blue serge, he was instantly recognisable for what he was: a law-keeper, an honourable member of society worthy of the respect that such a position affords. His mind, however, was not on the job in hand. Ever since his interview with his Chief Super, he had been worrying about what to do about Crusher Ericsson, alias Jeremy Small. He genuinely believed Crusher's story about how poor Rosie Little had died, and although Crusher had a volatile temper, he felt that her death had truly been an accident. He also sympathised with Crusher's unfortunate background: how he had been goaded into violence as a boy, a story not dissimilar to his own experience at school. In his own case, however, being of small stature and inherently of a timid nature, he had withdrawn into himself, whereas Jeremy had asserted himself physically and ended up embracing a very different path.

Crocker had submitted his report detailing the circumstances around Crusher's confession and arrest, but felt that he needed to see him, face to face, to offer support – to let him know that someone was on his side. Crusher was being held in custody in the police station, and although he, Crocker, could get access to the cells, he did not know whether to go as his *alter ego*, Fleur, or as himself, PC Crocker. He was in turmoil. He instinctively felt that if he went to see Crusher as Fleur, he would almost certainly be in contravention of numerous rules and regulations, and might even be discovered by one of his own colleagues. On the other hand, if he went as himself, it was possible that Crusher would recognise him, realise that he had been duped, and the knowledge that he had been wooing a man dressed as a woman might be just enough to make him lose his already tenuous grip on reality.

PC Crocker was also struggling with a number of other events of the past two weeks which he could not comprehend. Something about that guesthouse wasn't quite right. For a short while he had even considered that the guesthouse might be a brothel. But the Chief had put him right on that score and he now recognised what a ridiculous idea that had been. Something, however, just didn't add up. He couldn't tell exactly what it was, but his finely-honed policeman's instinct told him that all was not as it seemed in that particular neck of the woods – or in this case, the Common. Firstly, he was beginning to suspect that the nurse, the chambermaid and the French girl – who was also half-German and half-English – were not all that they purported to be. He was now harbouring a suspicion that they, too, were in some sort of disguise. 'Oh, my hat,' he thought, 'maybe they were also policemen in disguise.' Then there was the episode when the Chief was dressed as a cowboy: what was that all about? And how on earth did that man, completely naked, fall into a net? Something strange was going on, there could be no doubting that. 'Maybe I infiltrated some sort of undercover training camp,' Crocker thought to himself. His mind, never the most astute, struggled to make sense of all this information.

As Crocker trudged around the Town Hall, nodding politely at the dribble of voters as they entered, he came to a decision. He would go and see Crusher the following day and own up to not being a woman but an undercover policeman. He hoped the shock would not be too much for the prisoner. That course of action would also solve another problem which had been taxing him: what would he do when Crusher had served his sentence? He had, after all, promised to wait for him, and who knows what would happen when, after years in jail, he was released only to discover that the woman whom he had been yearning for – the person who had sustained him through the darkest hours of his incarceration – turned out to be a man; and a policeman at that.

Happy that he had made what he thought was the right decision, Crocker dragged his mind back to the job in hand and found himself staring unseeingly at a bicycle. He was at the back door of the Town Hall and was about to walk on to continue his patrol when something made him halt and look again. This was no ordinary bike – he took a sharp intake of breath. *Yes*, he thought – there could be no doubt. There, directly in front of him, padlocked to a railing, was a bike with a silver frame, drop handlebars and pink mudguards. It was the stolen bicycle, the one he had been hunting for, callously lifted without the owner's permission from outside the Herald Lounge Bar over two years ago. He had thought the case closed, the bike probably resprayed and possibly even sent abroad; but – here it was, as bold as brass, parked near the back door of Clapham Town Hall.

A wide smile spread across Crocker's face. 'Well! Well! Well! At last,' he thought. Crocker wondered whether or not to enquire inside as to who owned, or rather was using, the bike, but he couldn't take the risk of letting it out of his sight, not even for a moment. No, he thought, he would wait, and when the owner, or rather the thief, came to reclaim it, he would catch him red-handed and make an arrest. PC Crocker retired a short distance to the darkness round the corner of the building to await events.

Meanwhile, inside the Town Hall, voting was drawing to a close. The turnout had been low, with many Conservative and Labour supporters not bothering to vote. It was therefore not long after midnight that the Returning Officer was able to announce the results.

Only two candidates gathered on the stage to hear the results. The Liberal candidate, who was wearing a suit, looked slightly smarter than at the hustings and appeared confident, while Andy wasn't sure whether to look happy or miserable. If he looked confident, as though he believed he could actually win, any sensible observer would realise that he was pathologically unrealistic. On the other hand, if he looked as though he was anticipating failure he would be labelled a born loser – which, of course, he was – but that was the image he was trying to discard. In the end, he wore his normal vacuous expression, a feat aided by half a dozen pints taken with his party chairman in the Nellie earlier that evening.

Of the Martian candidate, there was no sign. On the chair allocated to him was a note saying that he was receiving a radio transmission from voters in another galaxy and therefore might be slightly late.

Having completed the count, the Returning Officer called the meeting to order and, after the usual formal preliminaries, began to announce the result.

'Stanley Howell. Liberal – four hundred and twenty-two votes.' The weedy man looked pleased and there was clapping and noisy celebration from around the room.

'Barry Walker. The Martian Party – six votes.' There was silence in the room.

'Andrew Norris. The BAD Party – five votes.' Andy could hear some dilatory clapping from where he knew Lucy and her friends were standing. 'I hereby declare that Stanley Howell is the duly elected council member for Clapham Common.'

Andy started to clap along with the audience. His thoughts were jumbled. While he had a great sense of relief that the whole sorry charade was over and, as predicted, the Liberal had won, in his heart he was disappointed that only four people, other than himself, had voted for him. As for the Martian party – to be beaten by a man who was clearly mad troubled him.

After some mumbling remarks from the winning candidate, the Returning Officer thanked the counters and then closed the meeting. Andy wandered over to where Lucy was standing with Lucinda and Rupert, her eyes red, a tissue in her hand.

Lucy hugged him and sobbed. 'Oh, Andy, that's just not fair: you were miles better than the others.'

'Life isn't always fair, Lucy.' Andy tried not to sound too relieved and adopted his good loser voice. 'The important thing is to have tried. That's my motto, Lucy. Try as hard as you can, and if you at first don't succeed – do something else.' Andy looked up at the ceiling and frowned, realising that the tenor of this epithet wasn't quite what he had intended, but he needn't have worried; Lucy wasn't listening.

'Andy, you're so brave. After all that hard work, leaflets and everything. All those long hours working with your team. It's just not fair.' Lucy dabbed her eyes again.

'Bad luck, Andrew,' added Lucinda. 'I thought you were great. I have no idea why you didn't get more votes.'

'It was a bit disappointing to poll less than the Martian Party candidate,' admitted Andy.

Rupert tried to be philosophical about the whole thing. 'Well, that's politics, Andy. Totally unpredictable; but, as you said yourself, you gave it your best shot. You can be proud of yourself.' He slapped Andy on the back.

'And you can fight another day, can't you, Andy?' Lucy looked at Andy pleadingly.

'Oh! I'm not sure about that, Lucy. The campaign has taken a lot out of me.'

'Oh, you can't give up now, Andy, you were brilliant. You just didn't get quite enough votes, that's all. There wasn't much in it and you were definitely catching up – another week of campaigning and you probably would have won.'

'Thanks, Lucy, for those kind words.' Andy looked down at the floor, adding sombrely, 'Now is a time for me to reflect on what might have been.'

Outside, Crocker heard the back door of the hall open as a dark figure emerged and headed towards the bike. After glancing left and right, the man began to unlock it. That was when Crocker left the shadows and silently approached man and bicycle. Once within an arm's length, he planted his hand firmly on the man's shoulder and said loudly, 'Got you. I'm arresting you for the theft of this bicycle from outside the Herald Lounge Bar approximately two years ago.'

The man straightened up and simply looked at Crocker in disbelief. Stunned into speechlessness, he offered no resistance when Crocker handcuffed him. 'You are not obliged to say anything, but anything you do say may be taken down and used as evidence against you.'

Just at that moment, the scene was illuminated as a flashbulb fired, showing a surprised-looking Liberal councillor-elect and an even more startled police officer.

TWENTY-THREE

The following evening, Andy was settled in the Herald Lounge Bar, pleased to be back to his normal routine. 'Zephaniah,' he said, 'I would formally like to thank you for being my agent and for your support during the recent, sometimes arduous campaign. As you may be aware, I was not elected last night and my ambition to make the world a better place has thus been thwarted.'

'Ah, man, I'm sorry.' Zephaniah sounded genuinely upset.

'I also have to fire you as I no longer have need of an agent.'

'Oh, Andy, that's harsh, I was jus' getting the hang of it: beginnin' to enjoy it.'

'Life *is* harsh, Zeph. That's the way it is.'

Andy picked up his copy of *The Evening News*, lit a cigarette and began to read. 'Here, Zeph, there's a report of the election.'

Zephaniah looked up from his copy of the *Racing Times* at Andy, whose face had gone as white as a sheet. 'What's the matter, man?' Andy continued to stare at the paper with incredulity. 'Hey, man, is you all right? You look as though you seen a ghost!'

'Look,' said Andy quietly. There on page two was a full-page picture of the Liberal MP being arrested, with the legend: *Shambles of Clapham by-election means Martian to be local MP.*

Andy then read aloud, 'Stanley Howell, newly elected councillor for Clapham Common, was arrested last night for the theft of a bike. According to Chief Superintendent Winterbottom, PC Crocker, the arresting officer, had been tracking the bike for over two years. The breakthrough came when Crocker, one of Clapham's top officers, who had only recently returned to uniformed duty after working undercover, spotted the bike outside Clapham Town Hall and single-handedly arrested the thief when he came to unlock it. The newly elected councillor, if convicted, may have to step down, and if so, the elected MP will be Barry Walker of the Martian Party.' Andy stopped reading and stared at Zephaniah. 'He was only one vote ahead of me; bloody hell, Zeph, that was close.'

'Hey, man, you didn't say the Martian man beat you.'

'Didn't I?' Andy feigned surprise. 'To be honest, Zeph, at the time I was a bit peeved to be beaten by him, but now I realise how lucky I was.'

'It's lucky you told Ted to vote Martian: otherwise you'd be a councillor by now, man.'

'I need a drink.'

'Thanks, man. Usual for me.'

Earlier that Friday, the Chief Super had summoned PC Crocker to his office. He was now standing to attention in front of the Chief's desk. The Chief got straight to the point. 'Crocker, you're an idiot.'

'Thank you, sir.'

'Why on earth did you arrest that councillor?'

'Because I had cause to believe that he had stolen the bicycle. You know, the one with drop handlebars and pink—'

'I know! I know!' interrupted the Chief Super, 'but you've arrested a local councillor, for God's sake, and somehow the press have got hold of it. Now I'll have to explain to them what on earth the force is doing arresting elected councillors all over the place.'

'But, as Lord Chief Justice Denning said, "Be he ever so high, no man is above the law", and a stolen bike is a stolen bike, whoever has done the stealing; if you follow me, sir. To my mind, this successfully concludes a two-year-long investigation.'

'I know, but if the Liberal resigns, we'll have a Martian for our MP.'

'That's not good, sir.'

'No, it's not, and it's all your fault, Crocker.'

'Could we say it was a case of mistaken identity?'

'You idiot! How can we say that when his picture, along with yours, is plastered all over the newspapers?' The Chief was silent for a moment. 'Anyway, the damn fool has actually owned up. He gave an interview earlier this morning saying that on his way home from the City one night it was raining and he gave in to temptation and simply stole the bike to cycle home. Apparently, he'd intended to return it next day, but took a shine to it. We've no choice but to charge him now.'

Crocker was thoughtful. 'That'll explain the sighting of the bike in the Clapham vicinity late last year.'

The Chief sighed. 'The events of the last few weeks have put an unwelcome spotlight on our patch, Crocker, and it's your fault.'

'But surely, sir, catching Rosie Little's killer and apprehending a bicycle thief two years after the event is exemplary policing: nothing short of remarkable!'

'Ah, yes. But questions are being asked about, the, ah, how should I say, the, ah, guesthouse, and its possible association with the unexpected withdrawal of two candidates from the election.'

'It's interesting you should mention that, sir. My policeman's instinct tells me that all is not as it seems in that particular guesthouse.'

'Oh?' The Chief Super feigned surprise.

Crocker glanced around the room and dropped his voice to a whisper. 'I think it may serve another purpose.'

The Chief coughed and muttered, 'Surely not. What on earth are you insinuating?'

'I think it might be an establishment for training undercover agents, sir.'

'Crocker, what on *earth* are you on about? You are clearly insane. Are you sure you're regular?'

'Absolutely – like clockwork, sir. No, I'm not convinced the residents are quite what they say they are. There are some unanswered questions there, I fear.'

'Unanswered questions?'

'Yes indeed. What is a chambermaid doing working evenings only? Why is the nurse never on duty in the morning, which I would have thought would have been her busiest time? And how on earth can a naked man wander into a net, and why was the chambermaid attempting to beat a confession out of him? Tell me that. Call me old-fashioned, sir, but these things just don't add up.'

'Crocker...' The Chief looked at his PC earnestly. 'There are some things which are – how can I put it? – not for the likes of you and me to know. They are classified – top secret. Some questions must never be asked, and that's all I can say about the guesthouse. Do I make myself clear?' The Chief tapped the side of his nose.

Crocker, still standing to attention, was at first completely taken aback. Then it slowly began to dawn on him that he had been correct in his assumption all along – the guesthouse was a front for training undercover officers such as those destined for MI5. He gave his Chief a knowing look, which made him appear rather simple, then tapped the side of his own nose.

'Mum's the word and Bob's your uncle, sir. No need to say another word. Completely understood.'

'Good,' replied the Chief, once more relieved by Crocker's naïvety. 'Well, at least the councillor's arrest has taken the focus away from the, er, guesthouse for the time being. Off you pop, Crocker.' The Chief looked up at his junior colleague. 'Oh, and er – keep regular."

***

The following Monday it was official and had been reported in all the newspapers. The newly elected candidate for Clapham Common had resigned. He had admitted that in a moment of weakness he had stolen the bicycle and commended the police on their tenacity with this investigation. He announced that he no longer felt he had the moral authority to serve the good people of Clapham Common as their councillor and therefore had resigned. Andy tossed the newspaper on to the table and picked up his pint. 'Well, Zeph, all I can say is – thank God for the Martian Party.'

'Here it is, twenty-to-one. It's a dead cert.'

'What's a dead cert, Zeph?'

'Martian Law.'

'What are you on about?'

'It's a horse, man, running in the 2.30 at Newmarket. It's an omen.'

'Put a pony on it for me, Zeph; for once I agree with you.' Andy looked at his watch, yawned and said, 'I'm off home. That bloody election has knackered me.'

An hour later, Andy pushed open the front door of Parkview and made his way to the lounge, where Lucy had installed a comfy chair for him. Andy considered it to be a very positive indication of the improvement in their relationship, and although not as comfortable as the old settee, it was much more comfy than the bar stool she had made him sit on for the last few weeks, and was fire-resistant.

Andy was surprised to find Lucy chatting to a man whom he recognised to be the Returning Officer. Lucy was bursting with excitement and, on hearing Andy enter the room, she leapt up from her chair and squeaked, 'Andy, you'll never guess what!'

Andy's heart began to race. He looked at Lucy and then at the electoral officer. 'Oooh, Andy, you'll never guess,' she repeated, literally jumping up and down with excitement.

'Guess what?' replied Andy cautiously.

'I think I should explain,' said the Returning Officer. 'Mr Norris, you'll probably be aware that the winner of the Clapham Common by-election has resigned as he has confessed to the theft of a bicycle.' The man's eyebrows lifted heavenwards, before he added, 'Which means that the candidate with the next highest number of votes is the winner.'

Andy looked at the man with suspicion. 'Yes, that's the man from the Martian Party. It's been in all the papers.'

'Well, not exactly. Strictly speaking, he should have been the winner as he scored the next highest number of votes, but when we tracked him down he said he was off to visit another galaxy and would be away for a while.' The Returning Officer sighed. 'He's been committed, which means *he's* not eligible to take the seat either.' Sensing the worst, Andy slumped into his seat and began to groan as Lucy continued to squeak, jump up and down and clap her hands uncontrollably. 'Which means, Mr Norris, amazing though it may seem, *you* are the duly elected councillor for Clapham Common.'

'Oh, Andy, isn't that wonderful? I said you could do it, didn't I? You deserve it after all that work an' stuff.' Lucy first hugged Andy and then the Returning Officer.

'Well, I'm pleased that at least *one* of you is happy,' said the official, extricating himself from Lucy's embrace.

Sensing Andy's mood, Lucy asked, 'Aren't you excited, Andy?'

'I'm just a bit overwhelmed. That's all.'

'Well, I could cry!' So saying, Lucy promptly burst into torrents of tears.

'So could I,' murmured Andy. The electoral official then shook his hand, muttered something about a travesty, then turned and left Parkview.

POSTSCRIPT

'Tell me, Crocker, what did Crusher—?'

'Jeremy, sir,' interrupted the police constable.

'Sorry. What did *Jeremy* say when he realised that you were a man?'

'Well, sir, to be brutally honest, I just couldn't do it. In the end I went to the cells as Fleur. I thought that discovering that I was really a man might fatally unhinge him.'

'Wise, Crocker, very wise. What did he have to say?'

'He said that I was someone he could trust. Someone with whom he could be himself and in whose presence he didn't have to pretend to be a heartless gangster. "I wanted to be with someone honest and trustworthy," he said, "someone who would believe my side of the story. You, Fleur, seemed to be just such a woman – even though you're no oil painting."' Crocker looked at the floor and stifled a sniff. 'I don't mind saying, sir, I was touched.'

'But that's a bit harsh.'

'No, I really think he did want a confidante, someone who believed in him – and he chose me.'

'No, you idiot, the "no oil painting" bit.'

'Ah, yes, that did rankle a bit, I have to admit.'

'Well, your testimony certainly helped him; accidental homicide seemed to be a reasonable charge in the end.'

'Yes, sir, and I'm sure he'll be an exemplary prisoner. He says he wants to be a social worker when he is released. Wants to help girls like the ones he met in the guesthouse.'

'Ah, yes, the guesthouse.'

'Mum's the word, sir.'

'You've become quite a hero, Crocker. You're hardly ever out of the press these days.' The Chief Super flicked through some newspaper cuttings lying on his desk. '*Undercover agent catches Clapham Common killer*; *PC Crocker grapples with dangerous bicycle thief*.' The Chief looked up at Crocker for a moment before continuing, '*Liberal councillor taken to task by lone policeman. Bike returned to grateful owner by PC Crocker*; *Country saved from Martian rule by PC Crocker* – that one's a bit far-fetched, in my opinion. Then here's *Crocker of the Yard gets his man*. And so it goes on.'

PC Crocker shuffled uneasily in his chair. 'Just doing my job, sir.'

'Quite. Well, off you pop.'

'Thank you, sir.' Crocker rose to leave.

'Oh, one final thing, Crocker.'

'Yes, sir?'